The Stone Soup Book of Sports Stories

The Stone Soup Book of

SPORTS

Stories

By the Young Writers
of Stone Soup Magazine

Edited by
GERRY MANDEL, WILLIAM RUBEL,
and MICHAEL KING

•

Children's Art Foundation
Santa Cruz, California

The Stone Soup Book of Sports Stories
Gerry Mandel, William Rubel, and Michael King, editors

Copyright © 2013 by the Children's Art Foundation

•

Stone Soup Magazine
Children's Art Foundation
P.O. Box 83
Santa Cruz, CA 95063

www.stonesoup.com

•

ISBN: 978-0-89409-031-8

Book design by Jim MacKenzie
Printed in the U.S.A.

Cover illustration by Rachel Stanley, age 13,
for "Diver," page 94

About Stone Soup

Stone Soup, the international magazine of stories, poems, and art by children, is published six times a year out of Santa Cruz, California. Founded in 1973, *Stone Soup* is known for its high editorial and design standards. The editors receive more than 10,000 submissions a year by children ages 8 to 13. Less than one percent of the work received is published. Every story and poem that appears in *Stone Soup* is remarkable, providing a window into the lives, thoughts, and creativity of children.

Stone Soup has published more writing and art by children than any other publisher. With our anthologies, we present some of the magazine's best stories in a new format, one designed to be enjoyed for a long time. Choose your favorite genre, or collect the whole set.

Contents

Twenty-Six

by Adrienne Hohensee, age 10

RAIN, TO GRACIE, had always seemed like the tears of hope. Instead of closing all the windows and playing board games, she walks half a mile to the nearest park. Running away from home was simple now. She had gotten used to it. Most of it was to the park, and most of it was in the rain. The two things just clicked.

When Gracie arrived at the park, it was almost always empty. Occasionally there would be a lone skateboarder, lining up the benches and crashing at the end. But on those days when the park was silent except for the pounding of the rain and the croaking of a lost bullfrog, Gracie took over the playground. It was astonishing the way she moved so well with the rain, silently but firmly. She looked as if a part of it. And the look on her face—so free.

What she is doing requires strength and endurance. But most of all, determination. She steps to the bar and grips it, but do you see that her knuckles are not white? See how relaxed she is as she pulls her body up in the air? Watch her chin pose directly above the fragile bar. Then watch it all tumble down, the bar

Adrienne was living in West Linn, Oregon, when her story appeared in the November/December 2009 issue of Stone Soup.

THE STONE SOUP BOOK

above her once more.

This act of power and grace combined continues twenty-six times. Her goal. She drops down, feet reuniting with the earth. The look on her face is the same as if she is a bird landing softly in the hills of heaven. She is ready. She has practiced for two months, ever since the last fitness testing. Then she had gotten four chin-ups, and with a heavy heart she remembers having to write that number on her sheet. Now she can write twenty-six and go to the fitness competitions. But there is one face she needs to see before all that is done.

"HEY, LOUIS! How many this time, huh, bud?" Coach Winters slaps him on the back like a long-lost buddy. The dumbest thing is that Louis replies in the same buddy voice.

"Twenty-four," says Louis, grinning across at his coach's amazed face, although he's heard and spoken the number at least a hundred times. They babble about the upcoming fitness stuff like it was the world.

But Coach has another period to attend to, and although he'll wait until the last minute to talk to Louis, Gracie knows he has to leave. She waits until they say goodbye and Coach walks off, whistling and grinning.

"So... twenty-four, huh?" she asks, trying out the buddy voice. She's just got to start drawling a little and smiling really hard.

He looks at her like she's stupid. Why would she be interested in what he was doing? But because he is a show-off and likes to tell people that, he nods.

She leans in close. "Twenty-six," she says, carefully enunciating each word. She doesn't leave yet, though. His expression is what she's looking for.

It's first confusion, like he has to piece together exactly what she's saying. Then it's obvious he's finding the difference between the numbers. When that's done, recognition—pure, surprised recognition—flashes across his face. All in a matter of two seconds.

She doesn't wait any longer and hurries away, swinging her books so that she looks relaxed, leaving him to contemplate.

GRACIE CAN'T FOCUS. It's the last period of the day, and all she can look at is Louis. He's angry, that's for sure. There's something else, too. He keeps looking up at her, and seeing that she is still watching him, turning away.

Louis is like a snake—if you challenge and corner him against a wall, he'll bite. Any little thing will tick him off now. He keeps frowning and glancing around.

He confronts her when the bell rings. She has been expecting it, and has the whole thing planned out.

"I can do it," he tells her. "Twenty-*seven*."

"Prove it," is all she answers, asking if he knows where her park is. When he nods, she only smiles and pats him on the back. Good sportsmanship. It can go a long way.

IT'S RAINING, again, when she arrives at the park. To her surprise, he's already there, huffing and puffing under the bar. It's not what she expected, but Gracie ignores that and keeps going.

Right when he sees her he flops down, as if he was planning what to do. "I can do it!" he says again, but he doesn't sound like he's too sure.

"Lemme see it," says Gracie, who is equally nervous. It's the first time she's let someone else be in her park, her *kingdom*.

The first few are easy—he does them good and quick, using energy to impress. He hits ten before he dwindles a little below the bar. His eyes flicker to match hers, and he sees her outstretched fingers—ten of them.

"Ten, keep going!" she calls, swinging her legs. The key, she knows, is to look relaxed and believe in herself. She shouldn't sweat it, but in the back of her mind, she finds the difference between the number he's on and twenty-six. What if she's really *not* ready?

He's got fifteen. Five to twenty. Then another six to twenty-six. Suddenly, to Gracie, the numbers feel small and weak, unable to hold the strength that Louis has. Louis himself, under the bar, feels totally different. They are painful and unwelcoming. He is going into new territory. But he's got the determination that Gracie has. Even if every bone breaks, he'll go on and smile at the end.

Twenty. He recognizes the number portrayed on Gracie's fingers. All of a sudden he's in the tens just like the goal. He hangs under the bar, fists clenched but a determined smile on his face. He won't quit on his dream, that's just not who he is. He passes his old goal and hesitates. He's never done more. But—of course—someone else has. So Louis doesn't stop. He keeps at it. Slowly, painfully, he sucks up a breath and pulls his weight up above the bar. His hands feel weak, but once again, his eyes are lit up with some magic that brings him ever forward.

Twenty-five. It's more than he's ever done before and he knows it. His arms look like string from the Dollar Store as he plops back under. You can see the white knuckles, the difference between Gracie and him. He lacks the grace that she has. But the power, the will—it's all there. He has strength. Gracie has endurance.

Suddenly he has the power and yanks himself up like a puppet on a string. It breaks Gracie's heart. That was her number, the special one she claimed as her own. He looks at her straight in the eyes. There are water petals clinging to her eyelashes, refusing to let go. She swears it is the rain, silently, to herself.

With the number in his mind, he pulls it up. Gracie's index finger cannot move. Now the race was not only a tie, but had a winner. Once again, Louis's hand would go up in the air, held by a referee's. Once again, Coach would smile at him and pat his back. It was as if nothing had changed. Gracie hadn't beaten the record. She hadn't done a thing. At least, she hadn't done anything he couldn't do.

Letting himself down, Louis stands there, panting. She gazes at him from her spot on the sidewalk curb, hugging her jacket tighter around her as if trying to keep the number close. But she knows as well as he does that it is gone forever.

He finally turns to face her. The sun captures his face in such a way, how the shadow of his nose fades over his cheek. She looks down.

"Nice job, Gracie," he says, and she knows he can distinguish the difference between the raindrops on her face and the tears. He's just trying to make her feel better. Gracie feels like she doesn't need his help.

"I can do it!"

He turns. She's standing up, looking at him with the magic. When she sees that he's watching her, she leaps to the bar. Unlike Louis, she takes her time. She wants to get this right.

Nothing's running through her head like usual. The days before, she would wonder how far she'd get in the fitness records. She'd picture Louis's face when she told him. Now, her mind is blank. She's in her own world now, back when the clouds were fluffy and the sunshine really was liquid gold. It was all too easy. There was nothing there. It was her and the bar. In a way, she knew Louis was standing behind her, counting, but he couldn't enter her world, the world where there truly were happily ever afters.

She's gotten to twenty-six with no trouble. It was like meeting the same stranger you met yesterday on the road—like all of a sudden they really were someone to talk to just because they appeared in your life twice. But all of a sudden, the world disappears. She's opened her eyes, and before her is the red setting sun, bold and miserable, taking a worthless journey across the sky.

Gracie watches the bar above her. Why? Why did she have to go *again*? Wasn't this the last one? But Louis has done it. So, ever so slowly, she comes up above the bar.

She hears a gasp. "Twenty-seven?"

THE STONE SOUP BOOK

She swings down. "You betcha," she tells him. With extraordinary beauty, as if she hadn't done a single thing to exhaust herself, she flies up to rest her chin on the bar.

Her breath gets caught. She's going to start crying—right here on this bar. But this time, of joy. Of pure, real ecstatic joy. Right up here, on top of this bar. Right up here, in the hills of heaven.

Falling Trees and Riddles

by Sabrina Wong, age 10

SABRINA HAD BEEN preparing for this for weeks. The small girl, with the statuesque figure and her hair pulled tightly back into a high ponytail, surrounded by a foil scrunchie, looked radiant in her amethyst team leotard. She sparkled, not so much from the glittery rhinestones sewn to her chest in a waterfall formation going off like a thousand shimmering flashbulbs with every move, but from a genuine smile that poured out, "I am happy to be here. This is *my* sport." Her cheerful face and the flame that burned brightly from the depth of her soul could light up any darkened corner. The day of the big meet had finally arrived!

Sabrina loved gymnastics from the very first time she entered the gym as a four-year-old. Back then, she was limited to somersaults, but she couldn't wait to catch up to the bigger, stronger girls who ran in compact, power-packed tumbling passes diagonally across the mat. She loved the meets. Sure, there was a lot of pressure to do well for the team, but pressure aside, the competition made her better than she thought she could be. All

Sabrina was living in Weston, Massachusetts, when her story appeared in the July/August 2009 issue of Stone Soup.

THE STONE SOUP BOOK

the athletes were there, to show off their best skills, and all the hard work they put into the sport. Competition brought out her best. Sabrina loved all the excitement and energy too, particularly at the start of each meet, bursting at the seams with anticipation. She loved hearing the national anthem booming up from the floor and into the stands. She loved standing shoulder-to-shoulder with her teammates, and the invisible, unbreakable bond that linked them together.

But soon, all eyes would be on her alone, when it was her turn to mount the balance beam—that four-inch-wide beam that appeared to float high up in the stratosphere among the clouds, although it proved to be only a few feet off the ground. The beam challenged her, looking menacing at times, even staring her down. But Sabrina would not let it get the best of her, not this time.

Using her warm-up minutes, Sabrina pirouetted perfectly on top of the beam, managing a full twist with her arms held high. She practiced her scale, elevating her leg in back of her, pulling her arms back into a wing formation, keeping her chest and chin both high. She was confident and ready. No doubt, this is the day she would get her Level 6 back walkover on the beam in competition. This was the only skill she needed which had eluded her. Some of her teammates of course had no problem with the skill, and others, like her, really struggled, needing to work hard at it. Still, she was proud of herself for taking calculated risks, daring to be better, and challenging herself to learn it. When her time came in front of the judges, she would need to bend backwards and kick one leg first, then the other, over her head, hanging for a second upside down, her legs in a midair split, then come up again in a lunge to balance herself, keeping both her fears and her poise in check.

The no-nonsense green pennant flag swiftly went up, signaling it was her turn. When she saluted the judges, her stomach started flip-flopping wildly. Sabrina wondered if anyone else could hear her heart thumping loudly against her chest wall.

First, she managed a first-rate scissor mount onto the beam, pointing her toes into tight arrows. She pictured her mom in the bleachers, holding her breath until she finished the back walkover that had given her so many frustrated practices, the skill that crept into her nightly dreams that seemed too eager to taunt her. This was her moment. Surely, with so much practice and so much coaching, she would do it now. She would taste victory— this time!

The moment snuck up on her. The time which held special meaning had arrived, no matter what the clock mounted high on the painted cinder-block wall announced. Sabrina stretched tall with her arms in the air overhead. Now, she thought. She carefully reached backward over her head, searching for that four-inch-wide strip of varnished wood. She found it. She pushed off on her right foot, keeping her eyes fixed upon the string of glaring lights overhead, trying to keep her position in a straight line.

But suddenly... oops, she could feel her foothold give way, and she was falling... falling... far down below into a deep, bottomless chasm. It would not be today that her spirits would climb to their summit. Her heart slumped and heaved a heavy sigh. She jumped back on the beam though, quickly, defying gravity, so as not to get another penalty deduction, and then finished up, holding her dismount for the required quantum of time. Her nemesis had won again.

"Better luck next time," she heard her coach mumble as she faced the disappointment pooling in her coach's bottomless black eyes where she saw herself in endless free fall. But Sabrina's own sights were set ahead on the horizon.

AFTER ALL the shiny medals dangling on thick ribbons had been given out, and with both the tears and thunderous claps now fading back into the background to lurk among the bars and beams, biding their time until their next invitation, Sabrina scanned the floor, hoping the beam was still free. *Yesssss*, she cheered in her mind. The next session wasn't about to start for another eight to ten minutes. There was still a chance. The gym was empty. The crowd had poured out lazily with magnetic feet, bottlenecking at the front door, like spilled sticky soda pop, and the new crowd hadn't been unleashed yet. Some of the conversation fizz was dying down. She knew she only had a little time to get back to work. She could picture her well-intentioned parents already waiting anxiously for her in the car, trying to find some comforting words.

Sabrina seized her opportunity, not waiting for any proctor wearing the signature maroon jacket with the pocket insignia to wave her off. Quickly, she did her scissor mount and promptly but gingerly completed the first half of her routine again on the apparatus. When it came to the back walkover, she looked to both sides. The gym was empty. Reaching back, she kept her focus. Her legs knew what to do. They almost seemed to lift themselves over her head, searching for the beam. She came up in a perfect lunge. Sabrina's heart soared to the rafters. There was no medal around her neck, no witness to celebrate her achievement.

"I did it," she shouted out loud. No one was there, ready to flash her her well-deserved score. A question bubbled up, taking shape in her mind without hesitation. If a tree falls in the forest, and there's no one around to hear it, does it still make a sound?

"Yes!" she answered herself out loud, but there was no one there to debate with. She had been puzzled by that age-old riddle ever since she first heard it, in third grade. But now, she knew the answer as sure as she knew her own name. "The tree hears it. The tree knows. Yes, it absolutely does! It does!" And sometimes, that's enough.

A Night for Soccer

by Andrew Lee, age 13

IT WAS BITTERLY COLD. Standing by the bench, our team huddled in a group, shivering as we listened to our coach. Gusts of freezing wind blew around us, pelting us with miniscule drops of rain that stung our skin. The moaning of the trees sung in the background. And the sky was dark.

I wrapped my hands in my sleeves, waiting as the referee walked up to the semicircle formed by the players. My teeth chattered as he inspected our cleats. I saw my mother on the sideline, wrapped cozily in her overcoat, raising an umbrella to shield her from the rain. She waved, giving me the thumbs-up sign, trying to encourage me. I smiled bleakly, and stomped the ground, trying to find some warmth.

The game started at the whistle. It was our last game of the season, and I was determined to end it with a victory. The field was ominous, huddled figures bent over, trying to fight the overpowering wind as they strove to control the ball. I quickly ignored my discomfort. My freezing arms could come later. Right

Andrew was living in DeWitt, New York, when his story appeared in the March/April 2009 issue of Stone Soup.

THE STONE SOUP BOOK

now, it was time to play soccer.

I sought for an opening in their defense, immediately attentive. Together, our front line moved in formation, advancing upon their defensive men. We followed the flight of the ball, waiting, like hyenas stalking a herd of zebra. And there was our chance. We pounced, each covering our own man as our striker attacked the ball. The timing was perfect. We quickly gained possession of the ball. I struggled against the wind, running up to join in the attack. Our striker swerved left, dragging two defenders with him. Branching off, our forwards ran up, threatening the opposing defense. The goalie looked nervously at our executed patterns. My breath came in ragged gasps, the cold air stinging my lungs. My lungs. They were burning, yet my legs were still frozen. I forced them to move. We moved in intricate patterns, each looking for the opening and the pass.

"Jimmy!"

A single word.

Jimmy turned and sent off a high cross. Perfect. I ran up with my teammate, zeroing in on the exact spot that the flight of the ball would end. The defender was slow to react, he turned and tried to intercept the pass. But I watched the ball closely as it came spinning down. The ball bounced once, and I saw that I was at the edge of the box. Possibilities sprang into my mind. I was suddenly overcome with indecision. Should I attempt a shot? Or get closer? I saw Jimmy running back from the sideline for a pass. My mom was in the background, yelling support, drowning out all the other people like only moms can do. My mind clicked in the split second it had taken me to assess the situation.

I forgot the cold. My lungs relaxed as I focused on the ball. I swung at it hard and low. My shoelaces connected with the ball as it swung in a frenzied arc. The ball shot off, and I turned to watch. The goalie was desperate. He flung himself at the incoming shot, holding his arms high. He missed. The ball was going past his outstretched hands, into the goal...

Ping! The metallic sound sang, announcing the verdict. The

ball bounced off the crossbar and into the air. The goalie recol-
lected himself and easily caught it. The crowd sounded as one in
their disappointment.

I shook my head in frustration, then turned to watch my
mom. I thought for sure that would have been a goal. My mom
smiled brilliantly, mouthing for me to keep trying. My teammates scattered around me patted me on the back, exclaiming
their confidence and faith in me. My mood lifted as my teammates' support soothed my dented ego.

Yes, I thought. There were still fifty-nine minutes to go. I
looked up at the sky, defying the weather as it continued to buffet
around me. Now the darkness and pelting rain only exhilarated
me. This was what I lived for. I turned and jogged back a few feet,
ready to receive the next probe by the opposition. The cold was
suddenly gone. And I was right at home.

Racing

by Isabel Sutter, age 12

I WALK OUTSIDE and feel the grass being crushed under my shoe. A light breeze teases the trees. The peaceful yard won't be this way for long.

"Come on, Klaire! Race me!" Sophia cries, grasping my hand and pulling me over to the edge of the grass.

"Only one race," I remind her.

"OK!" she says, itching to start.

"From here to Monica's driveway," Sophia says, pointing her finger at the gravel two lawns away.

"Got it," I assure her.

We take our positions. I crouch, poised, like an arrow about to be released from an archer's bow. My knees are slightly bent and my eyes are on the driveway. Sophia glances at me, and then models herself after my pose. She starts the countdown.

"On your mark, get set, go!" she cries.

We start.

I quickly zoom away, like a tornado whirling. My sandals fly

Isabel was living in Houston, Texas, when her story appeared in the July/August 2009 issue of Stone Soup.

off, but I haven't time to catch them. The world flies by as my feet leap over the soft green grass. It tickles my toes and scratches my feet. The air rushes by my head. My hair is flying in back of me like a banner. I keep my eyes on the ground so I can dodge the pinecones scattered about by the neighborhood squirrels. A smile leaps across my lips. I'd forgotten how happy running makes me. I reach the gravel and turn around. I'm far ahead of Sophia. A moth flies up from the dirt where I have disturbed it. I'm almost to the finish line and I slow down a bit, not a tornado but a zephyr now. I reach the driveway and stop, hands on knees and panting.

Sophia halts beside me. My hair is in disarray and my mouth is smiling, smiling wider than it has smiled for a very long time. "Wanna race again?" I ask.

Somersault

by Claudia Ross, age 12

OUR BOOGIE BOARDS went *bump-bump-bump* over the sand. The tide was high, and the waves were big. Just looking at them made me excited.

There weren't many people out today. Figures. It was two days until s-c-h-o-o-l started, the dry Santa Ana winds blowing in the hazy summer smog. My bathing suit was still sandy and damp from the day before, and oily black tar coated my bare feet.

We kept walking. We had to get past the rocks that shredded our feet. The beach wasn't sandy, or smooth. The stretch of coast was empty, and it was far from popular, being near an oil derrick and beat-up resort. This place was only full in the heat of early August when Malibu was too crowded. The beach had rhythm, personality: the happy loner that dallies; the dreamer that didn't care what the little blond gang of Barbies thought.

I could feel the hot sand through my worn black flip-flops. I started to sprint, eager. My blue Morey board, faded and battered, went *bump-bump-bump* in my wake. The string that

Claudia was living in Studio City, California, when her story appeared in the July/August 2009 issue of Stone Soup.

attached to my wrist pulled down a slope to the hard sand, near the green, murky water. It wanted to be in the waves, just like me.

I threw my towel down, kicked off my flip-flops. I ran down the beach, feet burning, dodging mounds of fly-ridden seaweed.

"Claudia!" my brother called. "Wait!" But then he was sprinting too, his legs matching mine, beat for beat, push for push. We dashed into the waves, a ragged thrill of energy soaring through me.

Shock. "Jeez, that's cold!" I said. *Bump-bump-bump!* my boogie board replied, splashing over the water's ripples. I waded farther in. Jack and I both gasped as the chilling water reached our necks.

We sank in deeper after we'd caught a couple waves. I could just make out a new group of swells on the horizon. Three feet, easy. Good-sized. As they came closer, my Morey slipped out in front of me. Sure, I thought.

"You gonna take it?" I asked Jack.

"Yeah, think so." He spun his board around, both of our backs to the wave.

It rose beautifully behind me, forming a perfect crescent. I kicked out onto my stomach, and the wave jolted me forward.

It all happened so fast: the wave went down with a crash, and my Morey shot out from under me like a man diving from a sinking ship. I was companionless. My stomach took a wrenching flip. Suddenly, covering my head (the one thing I learned from surfing lessons), I spun, some poor servant of the wave. I tried to force myself up, but white water held me hostage. Lungs bursting, I thrust myself upward. Air!

I stood, dazed and battered. I felt as if I'd gone through spin cycles in the washing machine.

But then my boogie board came floating towards me.

Bump-bump-bump! it said. I stared at it for a moment, and then raced back into the waves.

THE STONE SOUP BOOK

The Boarder's Battle

by Connor Nackley, age 12

As THE BOY dropped down from the icy ski lift and slid down the slope, you could already see the adrenaline pulsing through him like an aura of energy. This would be his last run of the year, and he knew it would be spectacular. As he glided over the snow on his board, he already knew which run he was going to do. With all of the possible choices, his mind was set on one run. The one run he could never do. This run was his enemy, a rival, a foe; he had to overcome the fear. His heart skipped a beat as he whooshed down the slope into the entrance to the run. As he looked down the slope he saw the obstacles, such as trees, rocks, and moguls, that he must overcome. He stopped. There was no going back now, he had to move on. His pulse increased tremendously. His eyes were bigger than his heart. This run was impossible! He had to move on or else he would be stuck on the mountain. He slid down the icy slope. It was getting colder by the second. His toes inside his boots were freezing, his jacket barely protecting him from the chilly winds. Snow started to fall from

Connor was living in Darien, Connecticut, when his story appeared in the January/February 2009 issue of Stone Soup.

the sky, the white flakes brushing like a small, soft cloud against the boy's face. Crystals of frost clouded his goggles, trapping him inside a different world of vision. He gradually picked up speed. The moguls were like jagged mountains shooting out of the ground. The boy slowed down and sliced around them. He was tired, and only halfway done. Fortunately for him, the rest of the slope was decently flat with only a few of the mountain-like moguls along the way. The boy carved and glided through it with extravagant ease. Then on the final stretch the boy wanted a thrill, he was going to try and battle one of the enormous moguls. He had enough speed, he was ready. He crouched down into a jumping position. As he hit the mound he lurched forward and flew three feet off the ground! The boy's adrenaline surged as he was in the air. He felt free and alone like he had never felt before. It was as if the world had stopped and he kept racing forward. The boy had finished his enemy. He had beaten it. He was satisfied and sad. He started to burst into tears, each drop like a drop of rain falling from his face. He would have to wait another year to feel free and energized. A whole year to challenge the impossible slope again. A whole year, yet he felt satisfied and accomplished that he had met his goal. He stopped crying. The boy said goodbye to the slope and went back into the lodge, ready to head home.

Daydreamer

by Hannah V. Read, age 9

SPLASH! A clap of water crashes to my cheek. But I don't even think about that. I think about how my arms and legs are moving—well, mostly my arms moving up and down but also going side to side. I feel like a bird, a bird soaring into the gray misty sky. The heat licking at my wings, but I am free, don't have to care about school or anything else. As I soar I see a medium-sized shadow sprint through the water as it sees my big body soaring above it. My eyes narrow in closely, trying to see the direction of the fish. I can feel it, and just as it is trying to turn around, I dive. Wings back, eyes forward, feet pointed towards the clouds, and I dive, I slice into the water like an arrow and catch my prey. I begin to eat it, and then I realize that I am still underwater. But then the strangest feeling pops over me, and I am not gasping for air. In fact my body begins to shift, shift into the shape of a fish, a silvery shimmering fish, gliding through the water, towards a group of smaller fish, doing fish-like errands. I swim around and around this area, and my tail begins to feel funny.

Hannah was living in Austin, Texas, when her story appeared in the July/August 2008 issue of Stone Soup.

Suddenly the oysters at the bottom sure look delicious. But, I need some air. I pop to the top, slapping my heavy—heavy?—well, slapping my heavy tail against the water. And then I realize—wait a second—I'm an otter. And suddenly every single oyster on the bottom looks sooo scrumptious. And then, I dive. Dive down deep, trying to get them, but just as I do that, a huge wave slaps against me and pushes me off course. So huge, the biggest wave I've ever felt. I swim back, forgetting the delicious oysters that just lay under my eyes. Forgetting everything except that my life depends completely on me getting out of this wave. I try kicking and steering my body to the side. I have never kicked this hard before—I will probably go limp. My heart nearly sinks as I feel the water steepen a little ways and turn my head to see a waterfall. My only chance of life is to find something that I can hold on to. And then, I see it, a rock, sticking up, just a little ways, I only have one chance to grab it, and I reach out and I let out the first real breath that I have taken in a long time, when I feel the smooth surface of the hard rock. But just as I shift to get into a more comfortable position, one of my paws slips and I hit my head on the rock. For a second, I feel pain, earsplitting pain, sucking my whole body into the feeling. But then, I remember. I'm just daydreaming, again. And I'm not an animal—in fact, I am a normal girl, and I swim back to my father waiting for me by the diving board.

Big Dreams for Number Seven

by Emma Dudley, age 12

WHEN ALICIA WOKE she first thought she was in heaven. Indeed, everything around her was white: the sheets, the curtains, the furnishings. She sat up in bed and instantly felt a shot of pain course through her knee. She lay back down and stared at the ceiling. Then it came back to her: It had been the fourth quarter with thirty seconds to go and Alicia's basketball team, the Bulls, were in the lead by one point against the Devil Rays in the championship game. The recipe for disaster. Alicia had been shoving with the other team's center in the low post when the shot went up from the point guard. She vaguely remembered jumping up against the center for the rebound... and then the other girl had hooked her knee and Alicia had collapsed to the floor. The last thing she remembered was her coach's worried face above her. And thinking that she had just got her game high record: forty-two points.

A doctor came in. "You took a nasty spill there. A ripped tendon in your knee. We've done the surgery."

Emma was living in Berkeley, California, when her story appeared in the March/April 2008 issue of Stone Soup.

"How long will it take to get better?" said Alicia, feeling dread seep through her chest.

"About a year," said the doctor, "just for it to heal, of course. After that you'll have to finish physical therapy. You won't be able to play next season."

Alicia blinked. Next year she would be a senior. Next year was the year she could get a scholarship to Duke, her dream school. Next year was supposed to be her year to be the best of the best and show it to the world. She was already the best forward on her team. And now she was going to miss her one dream she had had since she was eight years old.

"No basketball," she repeated.

"I'm afraid so. It's a bad tear."

Alicia sat back. That was all she could take in for now. She wondered if the Bulls had won the championship.

ALICIA'S MOTHER and father drove her home and helped her up the stairs of their house. She was still getting used to the crutches she had been given. Alicia then sat in a chair across from her parents. Alicia's family was not poor but they were not wealthy. She knew that her parents had wanted nothing more than for their basketball star to get a sports scholarship to one of the best schools in the nation.

"There it goes," Alicia said.

"There goes what?" Alicia's mother asked, looking sad.

"My opportunity to get a scholarship."

Alicia knew that her parents would try to make it sound like it didn't really matter. But she knew better than that. It was her father who had first told her about scholarships in sports and taught her how to play basketball.

"Alicia, you know that's not the only dream in the world. There are other things that matter. Like academics."

There it was. Her father was trying to put a good face on things. Her parents stood up and went into the kitchen.

Alicia hobbled upstairs and collapsed onto her bed. She

couldn't deal with the fact that she would probably not play any college basketball. Or make it to the WNBA. Just then the phone rang. Alicia picked it up and saw on her caller ID that it was her coach.

"Hi, Alicia. I thought you'd want to know who won the game," he said.

"Yeah, I do! Did we win?" Alicia crossed her fingers again, anxiously awaiting his answer.

"The Bulls won, Alicia. And I hope you know that we couldn't have done it without you. The Devil Rays couldn't get another shot off."

Alicia let out a relieved breath. But then again, she felt the same as she had before. What was the point if she couldn't play next year? "That's great," she managed to say. "Thank you."

"You know that there were scouts at that game. Forty-two points must have looked pretty promising to them, don't you think? How's your knee, Alicia?"

"I can't play next year."

"Your family told me. But today I saw this brochure for basketball summer camps for girls. They're looking for coaches. Sounds like just the thing you could do while still healing. I'll drop it off if you want."

Alicia said halfheartedly that it sounded great and then said goodbye. She then lay down on her bed again and fell into a dreamless sleep.

WHEN ALICIA WOKE UP she found the basketball camp brochure on her bedside table. She went downstairs to call Emily King, one of her teammates. Alicia needed to talk to someone. Emily said that she'd come over. When Emily came into Alicia's room she saw the camp pamphlet.

"This looks really fun," she said. "If Coach had recommended me I wouldn't hesitate! You should really do this, Al. It would be good for you."

"I can't even play next season," Alicia said. "How am I

supposed to wrangle a bunch of grade-school girls?"

"Come on, Al." Emily raised her eyebrows. "When we were in fourth grade you were the one who taught me how to play basketball."

"I still don't know," said Alicia.

"Well I do. Sign up for it, and if you change your mind I'll do it for you."

After Emily left, Alicia thought about the summer camp. Both her coach and Emily were right. It would be good for her to share her talent with others, even if she couldn't use it for herself. It might be fun, anyway, teaching her favorite sport to little girls.

IT WAS NOW late in June and the first session of the All-Star Girls Basketball Camp was beginning that day. When she arrived at the gym and saw all the little girls she was surprised to realize that for the first time since she had injured her leg she felt happy. She became good friends with all of the girls she coached.

At night she had long conversations with Emily on the phone. Emily said she thought Alicia shouldn't give up on her dream and to keep trying. Alicia found that she agreed. One day, after everyone had gone home, even the coaches, Alicia put on her old basketball shoes and shorts. Then she threw her old jersey on over her baggy white T-shirt. Then she picked up a basketball from the rack and threw her crutches down next to her shoes and sweatpants. Alicia then felt the pain, but she ignored it. She started slowly dribbling down court, with a huge limp.

Emily had dropped by to talk to Alicia. When she saw her dribbling down the court she stepped into the gym to see what would happen next.

Alicia was now at the three-point line, slowly inching her way towards the basket. Her eyes were squinted up with pain. She finally stood in front of the hoop and shot the ball up in a beautiful arc. The ball swished through the net. Emily slowly started clapping and shouted, "Forty-four points for Alicia Peterson!"

Alicia just smiled with tears pouring down her face.

Moonbeams into Eternity

by Colin Johnson, age 13

SIXTY SURFERS sat like giant black spiders, fangs bared, waiting to strike out and take one wave. Only one surfer would ride a wave at a time, which poisoned the air with the tense gas of ruthless competition. This was Trestles, a place where waves rolled like moonbeams into eternity. Because of this phenomenon, Trestles attracted crowds of people like termites to a rotting log.

My first time at Trestles was like a race in wheel-spinning mud. Of the two to three waves I caught, I only rode one all the way in. It seemed like every time I paddled for a wave, I missed the wave by five feet—just three more paddles and I would have caught each one. I felt frustration like an icy hot pad—cold with glum depression and hot with frustrated aggravation. Like a pot of moldy mush, I slunk back out to the treacherous takeoff zone on my surfboard.

"IT'S FIRING," Chance, my surf coach, gleefully shouted through the telephone. "The set waves are rolling in like

Colin was living in Laguna Beach, California, when his story appeared in the September/October 2007 issue of Stone Soup.

dinner courses at a five-star restaurant."

"Really?" I asked anxiously.

I was a little nervous about going to Trestles again after my first disastrous experience. At the same time, I was excited to give the world-class waves another try.

"Yes, it's two- to three-foot overhead, with an occasional four-foot."

I have gotten used to this jargon. One "head" is usually considered about six feet. So in this case, we were talking about set waves with an eight- to nine-foot face and occasionally one with a ten-foot face, which is the front of the wave.

"I'll pick you up after school," Chance said cheerfully.

Excitement bored a tingly shivery hole in my stomach, and my hands started to sweat.

Swookachsh!

Chance and I stood on the beach getting ready to change while waves like charging elephants rolled through the mossy rock point. Salty mist filled my lungs with new hope.

"This is it," he said as we began to paddle through the molten cloudy fluff.

As I sat in the lineup to wait for a wave, venomous glares from the salt-crusted spiders pierced me. *Who is this newcomer?* they asked with speculative beady eyes.

I tried to return their fierce stares, but failed and only managed a shivering glance.

"Whoa, that's a big wave," I exclaimed to Chance, pushing my electric-green board through the wall of blue gel.

"Shhh!" he replied with a cranky frown. "Don't say that."

"Why?" I asked, curious at the harshness in his normally calm and easygoing voice.

"I'll tell you later, but don't say that again."

A wall of sea glass danced toward me, and I paddled eagerly toward it with a salivating smile to ride its treasures. Excitement rattled my bones. There was no one to steal it from me. I was in the right spot and had the right-of-way. My silver fingertips shattered the smooth glass wall with repeated strokes of eagerness and delight. With a push from bubbly nature herself, I glided down the face of the wave, my fins slicing the shimmering sea like silver knives through honey butter. Suddenly, the silence was shattered by the slicing of yet another board. My screaming smile suddenly shimmered and then was blown out. Frantically, I shouted and waved at the rider to get off of my wave, but he just ignored me and pretended I wasn't even there. I tried to get next to him so that he would see me, but when I got close, he snapped a big turn and sprayed me in the face. Blinded by salty sea tears, I fell and smashed into the bottom of the sea.

"HEY, GROMULET![1] What's up?!" Chance cheerfully asked me a few days later. "Trestles is going off. The swell's picked up and it's going to be perfect after school."

"Can we go somewhere else?" I groaned. "Because last time I ended up at the bottom of the sea."

"Nah. We're going to Trestles. It's just that last time you did everything wrong. You have to keep your mouth shut when you go out there because if you don't they're just going to take advantage of you. For example, if you say the waves are big, they will think that you are a novice and won't let you catch any waves. Also, you have to strategize and get your spot in the pecking order. Right off the bat, catch a couple waves and do some good turns to let every one know that you mean business. Oh yeah— one reminder: Whoever is the deepest[2] has the right-of-way. So if you can manage to get the deepest every time, you're gonna get all the waves."

The next day at Trestles, I sat amongst the giant black spiders again. But this time, I was ready. When I was on the beach, I had told Chance, "If anyone wants to take my waves I say, 'Bring on the heat.'"

[1.] A gromulet, or grom, is a child surfer.

[2.] The deepest part of the wave is closest to the breaking section.

THE STONE SOUP BOOK

"That's the right attitude buddy," Chance had said, grinning.

Paddling up the point, I wore my stoniest face and said nothing. When the first couple five- to six-foot waves rolled through, I was as ready as a rattlesnake. It was my turn to strike. I nimbly paddled to the deepest place possible and dug my fingernails into the rampaging wave. Then with one last blast of effort, I stood up and claimed my first wave for that day at Trestles. I dug my fins deep and threw huge sprays. Out of the corner of my eyes, I saw the spiders staring their beady eyes at me. But this time it was not with a look of condescension, but with admiration and respect. My eyes shimmering with happiness, I paddled out hungry for a set wave. I waited and waited, letting many mediocre sets go by. Then the wave came. It was a rumbling twelve-foot monster. All of the waves before it had washed everyone else too far in to get in my way. So it was mine, all mine. With a few swift strokes and a squeal of delight I stood up on perfection itself. Silver drops of purity choked the air with the sizzling smell of satisfaction as I chiseled pictures into the canvas of dazzling droplets. Back and forth I swished, spraying clouds of frothy foam into the sun-bleached air. We talked very little, for our sunburnt smiles did all the talking as we walked up the trail and watched the evening sun melt sleepily into the snoring sea.

Ksssshhhhh...

Ksssshhhhh...

If at First You Don't Succeed, Try, Try Again

by Hannah Blau, age 9

Izzy AND HER sister, Natalie, stepped onto the asphalt at Bergman's Running Track on Norm Street. This was Izzy's favorite time of day. Quiet. The sun was rising. Izzy began to run, slowly at first, then speeding up. By the time she reached Natalie again she was at full speed.

"Time?" asked Izzy.

"Two-thirty," replied Nat.

"Yes!" Izzy exclaimed. "One more time."

The big race, three miles, was three weeks away—so far yet so near. Izzy spent afternoons practicing with her teammates. She practiced at the track near her house on Saturdays. Natalie, who raced for her high school, went along. Nat made Izzy feel confident. She was pretty and kind. Izzy admired her. She was a streak when she ran yet she was so happy and carefree. She would never be like Nat but oh how she wished. Izzy was also a little competitive with Nat. Izzy sort of thought it was good to be a little competitive. Maybe.

Hannah was living in Baltimore, Maryland, when her story appeared in the July/August 2007 issue of Stone Soup.

THE STONE SOUP BOOK

For the next hour, Izzy pushed herself to beat her best time. She loved running and the sensation of wind against her face at top speed. But she also wanted to win.

"Let's stop for a drink," Natalie suggested.

Izzy was glad. She was hot and sweaty. It was not an uncomfortable feeling, just a little feeling saying, "Mission accomplished." They headed to Brooks convenience store, where she bought a bottle of water. Then they walked up Norm Street towards home.

Every Saturday, Izzy kept to the same routine: She got up with her sister at 5:00 A.M., worked out at the track until seven and returned home a half hour later. At ten, her best friend Jessie would come by. During those hours, Izzy amused herself by trying to watch a movie (*Harry Potter*), or reading a book (*Harry Potter*) or fitting together the pieces of a puzzle (*Harry Potter*), though she could hardly pay attention. Finally, ten o'clock came and so did Jessie. She tapped out the secret knock, although it wasn't very secret anymore.

The door swung open and the two friends gave each other a quick hug. They grabbed some Power Bars and left for the pool. That was how it went every Saturday. Izzy liked it.

IT WAS the last Saturday before the race. Jessie had decided to join Izzy and Natalie for their Saturday routine.

"On your mark, get set, go!" instructed Natalie.

Izzy and Jessie ran and ran. On this morning, Izzy didn't notice the wonderful silence or the beautiful sunrise.

"Time?" Izzy breathed after finishing twelve hard laps, hopping from one foot to the other.

"Thirty-five minutes flat," Natalie replied.

"Not bad for three miles," Jessie said, trying to laugh. She was trying to be funny but Izzy could tell she was worrying about the race.

They practiced for another hour, trying. Izzy and Jessie were pleased. Better.

"You've got a whole week to practice," Natalie said. Her words were reassuring, but seven days didn't seem enough.

When they got home Izzy and Jessie were exhausted. No swimming.

IZZY'S TIME was improving, but butterflies were beginning to form in her stomach. They came flying in as the day drew nearer. And finally just when there was no room for another butterfly, not even a moth, it was time.

Izzy and Jessie arrived twenty minutes early, as did the rest. The girls greeted each other with chatter. They warmed up alongside the track.

Parents, teachers and friends arrived. Then noise.

"I'm scared," Izzy whispered to Natalie, who stood with her.

"Don't worry, you'll do fine," she replied.

Izzy took her place on the track.

The whistle blew.

Before Izzy could think, her legs were carrying her. Going, going, Izzy felt so tired and she began to slow. It seemed like forever before the finish line came into view. And it seemed even longer before she crossed it. Everyone else was there already, it seemed.

She had failed.

Izzy had thought she was a good runner and now what? Should she quit? She sat down with the rest of her team. She couldn't hear the loudspeaker as it called out the winners. Tears pressed hot behind her eyes. She looked down. This was more than embarrassing.

WEEKS WENT BY, races were missed. Practice didn't go well either. Nothing could comfort Izzy. She hadn't run for days. You'd have to be very smart to think of anything that would upset Izzy more than this, but your guess would probably be wrong anyway.

Almost every day Natalie would ask, "Are you sure you don't want to run today?"

And Izzy would always say, "Just leave me alone!"

One day, Jessie sat down beside Izzy in her room to talk.

"We've been losing all this time and if you don't start coming to practices *today* we won't get to go to the championship race. You need to be back. And I miss you with me."

"Huh?" Izzy was stunned.

"You're a great runner, Izzy."

"But I let you down," Izzy sighed, "didn't I?"

"You didn't. You were nervous. Everyone has those days. Don't let a silly little race tear you away from something you love," Jessie explained reassuringly.

"Really?" Izzy asked excitedly.

"Yeah," was Jessie's calm answer.

Izzy felt like crying.

"Thanks," was all she could say.

"So will you win?" asked Jessie. Her tone had changed. Now it was determined.

Izzy nodded. They hugged, then walked out the door of Izzy's house and headed to go—what else?—running. As she sprinted, wind whipping at her hair, a smile crossed her face. She was back.

IZZY AND JESSIE were the first runners at the championship race. Then the crowd and then noise. But Izzy didn't hear the noise; she was happy.

"On your mark. Get set. Go!"

Izzy knew exactly what to do.

She felt like wind. Sunlight shown on her cheeks, her heart bursting with joy. She felt as if she had already won. And it didn't matter anymore. *Is it possible? Am I more like Nat? Yes. At last,* she thought. *This isn't all about winning. It's about having fun. That was what Jessie had tried to tell me.* She felt the steady beat of her feet against the pavement.

Just then someone passed her.

"No," thought Izzy, "not this time."

And that's when Izzy ran.

Diamond Sky

by Sophie Stid, age 13

A SKI DAY means up at dawn. Dozy, half-awakening, drifting in and out of dreams. The flannel is warm, and the mattress is cloudy soft.

But it's up, sliding out of the billowy world of down blankets and fleecy comforters. Feet scrunch on the thick creamy carpet, hands reach for that glass of water you never finished last night. You sip it, slowly, in the dusky corner of the blue-and-teak room where the world is hovering between dusk and dawn. You gaze out at the pines, the softly falling snow, and the moose tracks like a finger drawn through icing. The room is dark and quiet, and the chair by the window is cold. Feet curl under, and cardinal birds flap in your stomach like it is Christmas. Your hair, morning-messy, falls over one shoulder. It's too early to think or do or say. This is the time to sit and sip and look out at the awakening world. This is the time for blue-and-teak quiet.

The snow ceases to fall, and now it's gray, but more like the English gray. Gray like a gull's wing, gray with snow waiting to

Sophie was living in Menlo Park, California, when her story appeared in the March/April 2007 issue of Stone Soup.

fall. And you hate to leave the chair by the window, hate to acknowledge the fact that it's 5:00 A.M. and you aren't sleeping, but you have to. So you slip on a sweatshirt, open the door to let in a slice of the rest of the house, a slice big enough for you to slip out. You walk across honey-wood floors in the kitchen, turn on the lights. Your sister Grace pops out from the pantry, making you jump.

"Never. Do. That. Again. Before. 8:00 A.M."

"What're you doing up?" your sister asks. She knows perfectly well, but she also knows that you are incapable of full sentences before ten thirty in the morning during vacation.

"Too. Early. Lemme alone. Pop Tarts. To pop. Shoes. To buy. Places to ski. Move."

She moves. Strawberry Pop Tarts are sweet and sugary in your hand, warm and golden from the toaster. You eat them your special way, peeling the icing off, licking the jam. Gross, but otherwise it's bad luck. Doesn't everyone know that?

The kitchen begins to hum, and it's still too early to talk, and you know people will tease and make fun of your inanimate self if you stay. So you go, curling up on the stairs, which is very strange, but it's too early to care. And then, when the gray gray sky begins to let down the snow again, people—girls—get ready. Ski boots and ski pants and parkas. Masks, which you never wear because you managed to actually find a cute ski hat in Teton Village last week, which is amazing. Soon you are in the garage, dressed and warm and with both gloves on, and you have no idea how you got there. You open your mouth to object, but someone—your older sister Lindsay—crams a scarf around your neck. You sadly realize that the cute hat is not on your own head, but when you begin to speak, you get a mouthful of red wool. So you kick Lindsay, and she kicks you back, but gently, because she is seventeen, and it's time for ski boots, ski poles, cross-country skis. Someone complains about you being so still, but you don't care as long as boots are on your feet and skis are on the boot and you actually have ski poles and you know today is ski day. Ski Day, talked about all your life, always secret, but today you find out, because it is the holidays, and the day before Christmas Eve, and yesterday was your thirteenth birthday.

"Hush! Hush!" The whispers circle around the drafty concrete garage, and boots stamp and your toes tingle. Grace and Lindsay and all the other cousins, aunts, moms, veterans of this. But for you—it is new, it is new, and you're beginning to wake up, and the cardinals in your stomach flutter once or twice. And you feel sorry for your sister Mimi, only ten years old, stuck in bed, but that was you all your life. Until now.

And the garage door opens. Creaky, groaning, *will it break?* One by one the figures file out, and when it is your turn excitement is salty on your lips. Skis slip from garage to snow, and you tilt your face up to the pink-and-gray sky, and the gray snow, and you laugh out loud, and it is like a baptism, pure and sacred and holy, snow on your face and shoulders, snowflakes melting on the black leather gloves. And because you can't help yourself, you catch one on your tongue, and the cold shocks. And you are fully, fully awake, for the first time in your life at 6:30 A.M., because how could you not be?

You follow everyone, side-slipping down the steep side of the driveway. She wasn't supposed to, but Grace, fifteen and competitive and a downhill skier, has been taking you outside ever since the snow started in November, teaching you how. You hear her voice in your head, *"Side, Sophie, side and back, skis straight, hold—do it right! Don't embarrass me!"* and you do it right, and Grace turns her blond head around to wink one brown eye. *"Good job, Soph!"* Lindsay catches on, the wink is obvious, but Queen Linds just laughs and holds her head higher.

You ski all day, across rivers and down trails and forging the trails on vast expanses of plains where you pick wildflowers in the summer. The world is different, transformed, under this mantle of powdery white, and it has been for two months but you have been too busy to notice. But now you do, and your breath is shallow. You are awed, aware of the sacred, quiet, still, pure beauty, and you want to shout. You want to shout, and run as fast as you can for as long as you can, spinning and arms spread wide, *freefreefree,* but you don't because that would shatter the sacred holiness of this place, and you would never do that.

After the lunch of salami and bagels you get tired, but you don't dare say a word. Grace is just ahead. You close your eyes, and ignore the frozen nose and toes, and the snow that lands on your nose and makes it colder. You tough it out, until you don't notice it anymore. And then you notice the gray gray sky and the pine trees tall and soft and powdered over with snow. And you are so far from all civilization, no fences, no houses or telephone poles or cars and you love it. But Grace is getting bored, so you tell her a quick funny story about school and everyone laughs. Aunt Emily, who complained about you in the garage, laughs too. "A comic," she says.

"No," your mother says, "a peacemaker."

"No," you say, "someone who is wondering when we'll get there." You would rather be a supermodel than any of those things.

"Soon," Suzy says.

You tilt your head back to look at the sky, and soon it grows dark, and the stars begin to smile through the snow.

"Soon," everyone is saying, refreshed and revived and exhilarated.

And then Amy and Sybelle and Mia whip a blindfold around you, and you scream, the world muffled to your eyes. Hands touch your feet, and socks are jerked off and on, and your feet recoil in the cold air, your red toenails very red.

"Come," says your mother. "Come." And she and the aunts take your hands, everyone else following. You're turned around, and the blindfold is taken off, and you look back into the corridor of pine trees down which you came, candles stuck in the snow, and it is so beautiful, so achingly beautiful as some things are, that the cardinal moves into your heart and fans his wings. And you're turned around to face where you're going, and oh my Lord!

An ice-skating rink is in the middle of nowhere, a pond really, iced over, with candles all along the edges and in the trees, and it is so crazy, so beautiful, you cannot believe what you're seeing, and the cardinal in your heart soars into song. Unconsciously you begin to skate, and you circle around and around, one leg following the other, effortlessly. Everyone else skates too, and you tilt your head back to laugh, but you stop midsmile because the stars! The stars are glinting through the black night sky, the cold hard black diamond sky, so sharp, so clear that you have to wrap your arms around you so you don't fall apart with all the raw, pure, wild beauty. Arms around yourself, skating in a circle, you don't know why or how or when you'll get home but for now all you need is this. This is enough, this is what you need. This is vital. And you hold yourself, and you shudder, and you finish your laugh, head thrown back, and drinking in the cold hard black diamond sky.

Bowl of Strawberries

by Andrew Lee, age 13

JACKY KEPT a steady pace, enjoying the scenery around his neighborhood. His old, worn sneakers kissed the asphalt every time he took a stride. The sun was out, and clouds scattered the sky like the stuffing from a ripped pillow. Jack felt his heart pound in line with his breathing. His legs slowly relaxed as Jack continued on his run. It was good to be alive and moving.

As he approached his house, Jack slowed to a jog and stopped on the front lawn. He sat down and stretched, easing the muscle he had just warmed up. The grass felt cool against his thighs. He took a sip from his water bottle, stretched some more, and walked inside.

"How was your run, Jack?" Jack's mother greeted him. "Was it hot out?"

"It was fine, Mom."

"Well, it's nice to know that you're not wasting this beautiful day."

Jack's mom had dark brown hair that matched her eyes, with a

Andrew was living in DeWitt, New York, when his story appeared in the November/December 2008 issue of Stone Soup.

serious smile that radiated her affection for her kids.

Jack plopped down at the kitchen table. Grabbing an apple, he opened the track-and-field magazine his grandfather had given him. It was a collection of a bunch of neat articles about the different events in track and field, tips for staying fit, and how to have a healthy diet. His grandfather had given it to him as a birthday present, knowing that Jack had recently made his school's track-and-field team.

"Hey, Mom? When's my next meet?"

"I wouldn't know, honey. Why don't you go check the calendar? I'm sure it's sometime this week."

Jack smiled. He threw the apple core into the trash and walked to the family calendar, tracing his finger over the paper.

"Hmm. My practice on Monday goes until 5:15 this week, Mom. My meet is on Tuesday. You're all coming, right?"

Jack's mom came into the room, wiping her hands on her kitchen apron. "This Tuesday? I'm sorry, Jack, I forgot to tell you. Grandpa said he wasn't feeling well these past few days. I have to go stay with Grandpa on Tuesday, but I think your dad might be able to come. I'm sorry about your meet, but your grandpa will have to go some other time."

"What's wrong with Grandpa?" Jack looked at his mother. "Is he all right?"

"Yes. He's just feeling a little ill. He complains that his ankle hurts more than usual. Why don't you go visit him after practice tomorrow? You could run there, and I'm sure Grandma will be happy to see you too."

"OH, IS THAT what she said, ill and not feeling well?" Jack's grandpa chuckled the next day. "I'm as fit as a violin."

When Jack gave his grandpa an odd look his grandpa merely said, "I never really liked fiddles.

"I just have to stay in bed for a few days. My doctor said my ankle's acting up again. Nice of you to come though, Jack."

Jack put his backpack down, relieved at seeing his grandpa

so well.

"Good to see you too, Grandpa. I'll have Dad tape our meet for you."

"Your meet on Tuesday? I haven't forgotten, you know, but I'm sorry I won't be able to come. But you know what? I used to be on the track-and-field team too, back in high school."

"Really?" Jack looked surprised. "You never told me that, Grandpa."

"I haven't now? Didn't I ever tell you how I busted my ankle?"

Jack shook his head no.

"Well. It was a very long time ago. My junior year, I think. I had joined the track-and-field team and was as excited as ever for our last meet. Let's see now. I was doing the long jump and the 400-meter dash. Huh, I never was good at jumping." Jack's grandpa sat up higher in his bed.

"My baby was definitely the 400-meter dash. Fastest on the team, I think, except for maybe the few seniors that were too lazy to sprint more than 200 meters. I was pumped that day, expecting to break my personal record."

"Did you?" Jack asked.

"Well, almost." His grandpa gave a sigh of disappointment. "I was coming around that last bend for the straightaway when I saw one of the runners from the other school gaining on me. I sprinted as fast as I could, but he kept on getting closer. I was about fifty meters away from the finish line when he closed in to just a pace behind me. Suddenly, I felt something clip my heel, causing my right leg to buckle. I tripped and fell hard onto the track. I tell you, it wasn't pretty."

"He tripped you?" Jack was indignant. "That guy should have been disqualified!"

"No one ever proved anything, and the official wasn't exactly paying attention," explained Jack's grandpa. "Heck, I don't even know myself. I might've tripped myself by accident. But I learned to accept it over time. After all, if life throws mushy apples at you, you can always make applesauce. Anyway, I twisted my ankle and felt a deep pop. Heard it, more like. I didn't feel the pain until five seconds later, sprawled there on the track. The people had to call 911 for a stretcher to bring me to the emergency room. Well, I could still walk then, but I had to be extremely careful. In my old age now it's been bothering me more and more. I spend so much time in bed now I wish I could have just finished that last race. If I had kept my lead over that kid and ended the race, I would still be up and walking now."

Jack looked in wonderment at the determined look on his grandpa's face. "The 400-meter dash? I'm doing that for Tuesday too, Grandpa!"

"Really now? Well, good luck, Jack. I wish I could watch, but I'm still expecting great things from you." His grandpa beamed at him.

"I'll win the race just for you, Grandpa. I promise."

JACK'S HEART THUMPED in his chest as he gulped. He repeated those words he had said to his grandpa just yesterday in his head. The day of the meet had come.

He was standing on the field, watching the events before his. The meet had started with hurdles, then proceeded to the 200-meter dash and 1,500-meter run. Already Jack felt his heartbeat speed up. His hands started to sweat as he gripped the bar of the bleachers. Watching his teammates perform so well made him even more determined to win the 400-meter dash.

The gun for the 100-meter dash rang out, and the flurry of sprinters took off. Jack watched as they pounded the track, pumping their arms and breathing wildly. They stumbled across the finish line, panting and gasping for breath. People cheered for their friends. And then it was Jack's turn.

"Calling all 400-meter runners. 400-meter runners, first call." The official spoke into his microphone, then loaded his gun with another blank.

Jack stepped out into the track, balancing his feet in his new racing flats. He felt light and full of energy. Almost feeling faint with a mixture of excitement and nervousness, he took his position in lane three.

"Calling all 400-meter runners. Four-hundred-meter runners, final call."

Jack stretched, took a deep breath, and shook out his legs. The runners from the other schools lined up in the lanes on either side of him.

The official came up to them for a brief explanation of the rules. Jack nodded dumbly. The official stretched the runners along the stagger positions for lanes two through six. He walked out of the way and held up his gun.

"Runners to your marks!"

Jack spread his feet apart, leaning forward.

"Get set!"

He tensed.

Bang! The starter gun went off.

Jack's stomach leapt to his throat. And then he was off, sparks flying off his feet. He sprinted fast to gain a bit of lead. Jack concentrated on his pace as he rounded the first curve. Now the race was just him, the track, and his own fatigue. Jack fought the tiredness that seeped through his muscles as he dogged ahead of his opponents. He strove to stay ahead as he coasted down the second hundred meters of the track.

Jack's feet pounded the ground as his breathing became hard and labored. His lungs were giving way. But Jack still did not give up. He saw the runner on his left inching his way up to him. How did he catch up? Jack increased his pace, sprinting for all he was worth.

Jack thought of his grandpa. He thought of the promise he had made to win the race for him. Jack's chest screamed as he continued his mad pace, but Jack's mind screamed back in defiance. He felt his feet burn as they dug into the shoes.

And now the runner to his left was gaining as the second curve played the advantage to the inside lane.

Jack felt his feet falter. His arms turned to stone as his

oxygen-deprived muscles started to shut down. The man on his left started to pass him. Jack's heart cried out. His grandpa would be disappointed.

But Jack was not done yet. Determined, he gritted his teeth, ignored his pain, and willed his feet to turn faster. The straight-away for the last 100 meters loomed up.

Jack imagined his grandpa tripping, the ankle snapping. He closed his eyes and ran as fast as he ever had. The soles of his shoes seemed to be burning off. The finish line was getting closer, but Jack knew he couldn't let up. The man to his left was neck-and-neck with him. At the last few meters, Jack summoned all his energy into the final strides, breaking the finish line just as his body gave up.

But it had not been enough.

He stumbled, and then crashed. Jack heaved as his chest strived for oxygen. The track was hot, and he lifted his face. Second place. Jack felt as if he had failed. Everything was blinding. He saw dark, and a crazy, dizzying feeling swallowed his mind. All he could think of was the promise he had made to his grandpa. Second place. But suddenly, his grandpa appeared in his dream.

"Grandpa?"

Jack's vision cleared and he saw his grandpa in a wheelchair next to him on the grass. "Is that really you?"

"You bet it is," said his grandpa cheerfully. "I was feeling chipper so I decided to persuade your mom into hightailing down to your meet. That was a nice race, Jack."

Jack felt tears spring to his eyes. "But I lost, Grandpa. I promised you I would win."

He sobbed, grief overcoming his exhausted body. He saw a few parents staring, but he didn't care.

"Jack." His grandpa looked him straight in the eye. "I'm proud of you. Never forget that. I wanted to come to thank you personally for finishing my race. I owe that to you. You did well to place second. And now I want you to enjoy it. Life's just a bowl of strawberries, you know."

Jack smiled through his tears. His grandpa was right. It had been a good race.

Tested Dreams

by Dominique Maria Spera, age 13

A NINE-YEAR-OLD girl sat on her parents' bedroom window seat looking out at the stormy, gray sky. It's going to rain, thought the girl. It's going to mimic how I feel. Slowly the girl lowered her tear-filled brown eyes to her right knee. It felt a little better now, but just a day earlier she had to be carried off her beloved tennis court because her knee had been so inflamed it could not support her weight.

Blinking back her tears, the girl looked back out the window. It was now pouring so hard that not even the other townhomes across the street could be seen. The girl smiled briefly. Let it rain, she thought as her mind wandered back to yesterday's tennis match.

It had been a tough match. No doubt about that. She was playing a boy almost twice her age when a searing pain went through her right knee. Thinking she had just stepped wrong, she shrugged it off like any other self-respecting tennis player would. That was a mistake. A mistake she would have to live with

Dominique was living in Altamonte Springs, Florida, when her story appeared in November/December 2006 issue of Stone Soup.

THE STONE SOUP BOOK

for a long time.

As the match continued, the pain in her right knee worsened, but she fought through it. In her mind, there was no greater shame than saying the words "I quit." The girl looked down at her knee and wiped a stray tear off her face. That had been her second mistake. She had not believed in the saying, "Discretion is the better part of valor," and for that she had paid.

Resuming her gaze at the pouring rain outside the window, she remembered the last point in the match. The point when she knew she had to stop. She remembered swallowing hard as she readied herself for the return of service while trying to block out the throbbing pain from her knee. She just had to finish the game. She just had to play one more point.

"No, I didn't," whispered the girl, "I didn't have too. I could have just walked away and retired from the match then and there." The girl sighed as she repositioned herself on the ledge. "But I couldn't," as she paused, a tiny flicker of flame briefly appeared in her brown eyes, "I just couldn't do it. I couldn't give up." Still maintaining her gaze out the window, she recalled the memories of that one last point. How she had painfully dragged her leg to return the tennis balls. How she eventually had made an error ending the point and the game.

But even with all that, the girl thought the toughest thing in the match was to say the words "I retire" to her opponent. She had never quit before, and she hoped she would never have to again. Those two little words were painful to say, almost more painful than her knee, and they had left a bad taste in her mouth.

The girl looked away from the window to look at her injured knee. Oh, how could you do this to me! she thought venomously. Who knows when I can play again because of you! The girl swallowed hard, fighting to hold back her tears. She loved tennis and who knew how long this injury, this first injury, would keep her away from her beloved sport.

Then, for the first time, it hit her. Injuries are a part of sports. They are what make you or break you. They define your career. They test your love for the game and the will that you have for fulfilling your dreams. And, in some cases, they can even force you to form new loves and new dreams.

But this was not truly a bad injury. It was one of those injuries that was to test her. Test her love and devotion to her tennis. And, it was with this new realization that she made another one. If she truly loved tennis, if she truly wanted to play again, she would not be sitting up on this ledge moping, but downstairs icing her knee and preparing for her eventual return to the tennis court.

"I will come back," began the girl strongly. "No matter what's wrong with my knee, I won't let it stop me." The girl then raised her head to once again look out the window. The pouring rain had stopped, and amongst what remained of the ugly, gray clouds, a beautiful rainbow was forming in the sky. The girl smiled at this, for now the sky was mimicking her new feelings; feelings not of despair or of self-pity but of strength and determination to return, no matter what, to her precious sport.

"And when I come back," continued the girl softly, an indescribable glow in her brown eyes, "I'm going to be better than ever." And with that the girl got up off the ledge and headed downstairs to get ice for her knee, for now instead of moping she would work as hard as she could to really come back better than ever.

Adrian

by Katie Russell, age 12

IT WAS a beautiful afternoon in August; it was slightly breezy and there wasn't a cloud in the baby-blue sky. School started in two weeks and the kids in my neighborhood were going all out, trying to squeeze all the fun they could into those last precious hours in the park. The kids in sixth grade were especially outrageous. You weren't allowed to play in the park as soon as you entered middle school. It was an unwritten law set down by years of sun-streaked kids coming and going.

This was my last summer. My friends and I woke up early each morning and came home late each night. Dusty, tan and happy, we'd crawl into our beds without bothering to change.

It was softball that I was most interested in. Softball. We were obsessed. No matter how many times we'd been told to by well-meaning mothers, we wouldn't change our interests to something more feminine, like makeup, or clothes. The mothers would sigh and shake their heads, hoping that we would come down to earth by the time middle school rolled around.

Katie was living in Charlotte, Vermont, when her story appeared in the September/October 2004 issue of Stone Soup.

There were five of us; me, Amy, Francine, Kath, and Becca. Amy was short with red hair and tons of freckles. She was short-tempered, but if you got on her good side, she was as kind as could be. Francine had long blond-brown hair that fell to the middle of her back. She was the quiet one among us, though compared to most people she was incredibly loud. Kath, or Kathleen, with brown hair cut close to her head, was the sports player among us. We all played softball, but she played every possible sport that she could. Becca, with black hair that was always pulled back into a ponytail, was the intellectual one. For some reason, she had been born with a gift for math, something that none of us understood. We were best friends, and we thought that we would never accept another person into our group.

The softball field that we played on was old, so old that our grandparents remember playing on it. There had been several suggestions to tear it down and build a couple of soccer fields in its place. They had been solidly refused, not only by us, but also by more than half the adults in the town, people who had grown up with it there.

There were no dugouts like the newer fields, but it didn't matter to anyone. The grass was mostly brown with scattered bits of green mixed in; cigarette butts were more common than either color grass. The dirt that formed the diamond had not been replaced in a while, making the ground as hard as cement. All in all, the field was a waste of space, but it was perfect for our purposes.

Today we were, like all other days, playing softball. It was windy and dirt was getting thrown up in our eyes. There were enough of us only to have one pitcher, one batter, a first baseman, a shortstop and an outfielder. This wasn't enough, especially toward the end of the summer, when we'd had two and a half months to practice, but we worked through it all, adapting the rules to fit our purposes.

We were years older than anyone else, most of the kids having already adjusted into the normal world according to their

THE STONE SOUP BOOK

proud parents. We were labeled The Outcasts and spit on by kids three years younger than us. We didn't mind the spitting or the names, but if a kid ticked us off, a bloody nose solved matters temporarily.

Today Amy was pitching and I was supposed to be batting, when I saw a figure coming toward us. I turned to look, stunned. Nobody, absolutely nobody, ever came to see us. We were used to it.

This was someone new. It had to have been, I thought. A ball whizzed by my head and I turned to glare accusingly at Amy. She shrugged, then laughed.

"Served you right!" she called.

I stuck out my tongue and turned back around, letting go of the bat. It slid to the ground with a soft tap. The figure was closer now and I could tell it was a girl. The rest of my friends saw what I was looking at and walking toward me. We gathered around home plate, all glaring at this newcomer.

The girl was tall, over five feet, an accomplishment in us since we'd all been born into short families. Her hair was dark brown, pulled back roughly from her face and tied in a ponytail. The baseball cap that was shoved on her head was dark blue. She was wearing a dark pink tank top, with light pink shorts.

It was Francine who spoke first. "Nice outfit."

Amy spat rudely at the new girl's feet. "I think the mall's that way." She gestured with a tip of her head.

The new girl stared steadily at them with dark brown eyes, reminding me of a trapped deer.

"My name's Adrian. I came to play softball." Her voice was quiet, but she sounded self-assured. For some reason, I wanted desperately to save this girl from the fate that she was accepting unknowingly.

"OK, you can bat," I said quickly. Francine looked at me strangely, but I shrugged.

Francine shrugged too. "Why don't you play catcher, then?" she suggested. I nodded mutely.

We walked back to our positions. I crouched behind the plate. Adrian picked up the bat I'd dropped. She clamped her hands around it, squeezing hard until her fingers were striped red and white. Her fingernails were painted a light green, but it had started to chip away.

Eventually, she shuffled up to the plate. Amy threw the ball perfectly. It was going to be very hard to hit, I thought. I doubted Adrian would even swing. Adrian looked carefully at the approaching ball, then swung powerfully.

With a resounding crack, the ball met the bat and it flew farther than we'd ever, in five years, hit a ball. It flew over the brown wood fence that bordered the softball field and toward the house nearby. There was the sound of splintering glass and a female voice yelling at the top of her lungs.

Adrian tossed the bat aside and loped carefully around the bases. We all stared at her as she crossed home plate. She blushed red.

"What?" she murmured.

"Hey," I said finally. "My name's Sammy."

The Baseball

by Katie Russell, age 13

ADRIAN STARED at the ball in her hand. It was old, obviously well-used and well-loved. Dirt and grass had been ground into it, its once shining whiteness now a muddy, undetermined brown. The laces had been worn down, rough and rusty red. When Adrian held the ball, her hand could feel familiar bumps and dents that had come from years of use.

Adrian could remember when her sister, Jenna, had first handed her the ball and taught her how to play baseball. The ball had been new then, just-bought-from-the-store new. Its creamy outside had promised exciting adventures that the two would face. Adrian loved the ball.

It had been years since Adrian last played baseball. Two years and four months to be exact. Ever since her move from Boston, Adrian had stayed away from baseball. It wasn't that there weren't any baseball teams in New York City. There were. And it wasn't because she wasn't a very good player. She was. It was that playing baseball brought back painful memories of Jenna, and when

Katie was living in Charlotte, Vermont, when her story appeared in the September/October 2006 issue of Stone Soup.

they'd played together and had fun.

Jenna was one of those older sisters that everyone wishes they'd had. Beautiful, carefree, and good at everything, it was Jenna who'd introduced Adrian to everything she loved now.

When Adrian was nine, Jenna found drugs and alcohol. Adrian watched as Jenna drew away from her, slowly at first, then faster and faster until all Adrian had of her confident older sister was a shadow of a memory and a forlorn baseball. Adrian's parents, unsure how to deal with this new daughter they now had, divorced, and Adrian was sent to live with her father in New York, while Jenna lived with their mother in Maryland.

Adrian hadn't seen Jenna since the divorce, but she dreamed of someday going to Maryland and asking to play baseball or to talk with her older sister.

Adrian, thinking of this, gripped the ball hard and bit her lip, trying to keep the tears from spilling out. Once she got herself firmly under control, Adrian glanced around. She was sitting against the base of a tall tree in the park, surrounded by laughing, talking, happy children. In the distance, there was even a small group of girls playing softball.

The air smelled sweetly of cut grass and the cool breeze swept over Adrian's face, blowing her dark brown hair into her face. The massive roots of the towering oak she was leaning against dug into her back and she could feel the rough bark on her bare arms. A woman with her auburn hair pulled back into a ponytail ran by on the dirt path inches to Adrian's left, humming quietly to herself. Adrian smiled as she watched one of the softball players hit the ball deep into center field.

Jenna would love it here, Adrian found herself thinking, unconsciously scratching at her light green nail polish. She would immediately ask to go play with the girls playing softball, no matter that she was at least five years older than them and that she actually played baseball. The girls would be so impressed by Jenna that they wouldn't mind if her tagalong sister joined them. They might even notice Adrian once in a while.

THE STONE SOUP BOOK

Suddenly Adrian realized that the Jenna of today, the Jenna she would meet if she ever went to Maryland to visit, wouldn't care about things like this. She didn't care about baseball, about parks, about impressing softball players, and she didn't care about Adrian.

Adrian leapt to her feet and threw the ball far off into the deep, green woods. Then she walked down the dirt path towards the softball players.

Note: This story is a sequel to "Adrian," which appeared in the September/ October 2004 issue of Stone Soup.

Thirteen and Still Feeling Lucky

by Matthew Taylor, age 13

I LEANED BACK in the cushioned seat of the gondola. I looked over at my close friend and mountain bike riding partner Daniel Vest. Dirt smudges ran across his face, and his clothes had a tint of brown on them. Both of our shirts were drenched with sweat.

I drummed my fingers on the seat. Outside, the wind howled at us as the gondola took us to the top of Mammoth Mountain. Daniel and I had been riding cross-country trails all day to train for our next race, and to finish the day off, we were going to ride the world-famous downhill course Kamikaze. It drops from a summit of 11,053 feet to 8,900 feet in about seven minutes, riding at a medium pace.

Daniel rode a Specialized Hard Rock, a 24-speed hardtail and an all-out cross-country bike. I had a Schwinn Rocket 88, a 27-speed full-suspension bike. It was also a cross-country bike. At the time, we were both saving up for downhill bikes so that we could each have one bike for downhill and free riding and one

Matthew was living in Mammoth Lakes, California, when his story appeared in the July/August 2003 issue of Stone Soup.

THE STONE SOUP BOOK

bike for cross-country; however, we couldn't wait until we had the right equipment. The Kamikaze's draw was too powerful. I looked out the window. Trees stretched out for miles and miles, and they could be seen all the way to the White Mountains.

The gondola rumbled and shook as we entered the station at the peak of Mammoth's height. The doors opened with a sound like the release of a cap on a soda bottle.

Daniel and I grabbed our glasses, stepped out of the gondola, and wheeled our bikes out of the station and down the stairs. A cold wind blew through the air and moaned in my ears. A dust devil swirled through the air, causing all of the tourists who were taking the scenic gondola ride to gape and point. I looked over the barbed-wire fence which separated the level ground from a section of Kamikaze. The wide course was windswept, and rocks littered it.

Daniel and I clipped into our pedals and rode toward the start. A wooden sign read *Kamikaze,* and right next to the name of the course there was a black diamond. My stomach knotted up. Should we be doing this? It was a pro downhill course, and we were only thirteen. No, I said to myself, I can't chicken out now. I've just got to do this.

We turned and began our descent.

One minute later, we were speeding down the course side by side. Unlike the sheltered cross-country courses, trees were nowhere to be found except in the distance since the course was above the tree line. There were, however, plenty of rocks. My shocks rocketed up and down. My fingers were sore because of their position on the brakes. I had to be ready for anything. My knees moved in harmony with my shocks. The wind blew into our faces and moaned in our ears, but neither of us was daunted.

I saw a bump throw the back of Daniel's bike into the air. His back tire came down crooked, but he shifted his weight and corrected it just in time. He then began a right turn which took us into another straight downhill section. I shifted my weight toward the back tire so that I didn't lean forward too much. We leaned into another right turn. Pink flags fluttered in the wind to our left.

I sighed in relief. This was the last part of the course. We were finally done. I pushed my pedals as I tried to catch up to Daniel, my bike wobbling from the sheer speed of it all.

"Whoa!" Daniel shouted. He leaned into a hard left turn and was then out of sight. Right ahead of me lay a series of sandy ditches. That was why Daniel had turned so suddenly. I, however, couldn't turn. If I turned right, I would just hit more sand. If I turned left, I would hit the metal pole that supported the pink flags. I stared ahead, frozen. A bump knocked my hand off its resting position on the back brake. I braced myself for the impact. I would have to do whatever I could to avoid injury. My front tire dug into the sand, and my bike immediately stopped. I, however, kept moving. My stomach lurched as my body threw itself over the handlebars. There was a snap as my clip-in shoes tore out of the pedals. My arms flailed as I flew through the air. My legs jutted upward. I was in the same position a swimmer is in as he dives into the water, but my hands weren't in front of my head. My head slammed into the ground. Bright lights erupted in my eyes. I kept rolling and rolling until the sand finally stopped me. I heard Daniel shout something, I couldn't tell what, as he dropped his bike and sprinted toward me. My head burned, and it felt as if it were swelling inside my helmet. I unbuckled my helmet and threw it to the ground.

"Are you OK?" Daniel asked.

"Yeah, I'm fine," I replied. I put my hand in my hair. Rocks littered it, and dirt was smeared all over my shirt. I sat there for about a minute.

Finally, after he asked if I was OK again, Daniel suggested that we get to the bottom. I nodded.

WE SAT on a bench outside of the main lodge. I looked around at all of the tourists who climbed the climbing wall and rented mountain bikes. I rubbed my head. That had been

THE STONE SOUP BOOK

a pretty hard fall. My head still hurt, but it should since the fall was only about—how long ago was it? I thought about it. Why couldn't I remember? I had fallen on...

"Oh, no," I said.

"What?" Daniel turned to me.

"I... I don't remember where I fell, or when I fell, or anything." My voice trembled. "All I know is that I did fall."

"Do you remember riding the gondola?" Daniel asked.

"We rode the gondola? We didn't ride the gondola, did we? We just got here, right?" Everything between waking up this morning and now was nothing but empty space. I began shaking.

"We've been up here all day!" Daniel said, his voice rising.

"Where did I fall?" I asked.

"Kamikaze," Daniel answered.

"But that's a downhill course, and it's way up there," I said, pointing to the top of the mountain.

"I know," he said. "But we wanted to do it all day, so we did."

I shook my head in disbelief. All right, I thought, I need to figure out what I remember. I need to spit out facts. Just facts.

"I'm Matthew Taylor," I said. "And you're Daniel Vest. My mom is Cathy Enright. My dad is Gary Taylor. My step-dad is Greg Enright, and my stepbrother is Matt Enright. We live in Mammoth Lakes, California. My birthday..." I paused. When was my birthday? "My birthday is September 11."

"No, it's not," Daniel turned to me. "You're a little more than a week younger than I am, and my birthday is September 14."

"Oh, no," I said, shaking my head. What if I forget all kinds of important things? What if I forget my friends' names or things that have happened to me?

Calm down, I said to myself. So far you only forgot your birthday and most of today. It'll probably come back soon.

I saw Daniel's eyes darting around. A woman walked by. He ran up to her.

"Excuse me," he said, "do you think there's a doctor here?"

"Yeah," she said, pointing to the Adventure Center. "There's probably one in there."

THE REST of the day consisted mainly of questions being asked over and over. I had to say my real birthday about fifty times, but it turned out that I had just had a mild concussion. That night as I lay in bed, still unable to believe that I had actually lost my memory for a while, I began to wonder why I mountain biked despite the obvious risks. I always heard about really hard crashes, and I had just had one. So what kept me going? I thought about it until I saw the answer. It's the thrill of going fast, the adrenaline rush of hitting a drop-off, the muscle burn of going up a hill, the technicality of the rocky, sandy, steep sections, and the passion that I feel as I push the pedals. Put simply, it's the love of the sport that keeps me going. It's the continuation after hundreds of crashes that separates the real mountain bikers who love the sport from the people who cry and put their bike away after a little scrape on the knee. Despite the hardest crashes that I will take, I have the privilege of being able to call myself a mountain biker, and because of that, I'm thirteen and still feeling lucky.

Revenge Is Bittersweet

by Molly O'Neill, age 13

IT WAS a perfect shot. I was standing across the driveway from the basketball hoop—just beyond where the three-point line would have been—and Matt, who was rebounding, gave me a nice crisp bounce pass. I bent my knees and sent the ball arching beautifully towards the basket. Everything about the shot was perfect—the timing, the follow-through, and the soft *swish* of the ball falling through the net.

And for once even Matt didn't have any wisecracks to make. He just caught the ball and turned around to make a lay-up, which was about the highest compliment I could get from my older brother because I knew he would have tried the shot if he thought he had a chance at making it.

Just then Carla's dad pulled his silver Saab into the driveway. Matt tossed me the ball. "You'll do great," he said.

I hopped into the back seat of the car. Carla stopped listening to her MP3 player and said, "Nice shot."

"Thanks." I grinned. Carla knew how to give a compliment,

Molly was living in New Canaan, Connecticut, when her story appeared in the July/August 2006 issue of Stone Soup.

how to make a casual remark into the most beautiful music. That was part of the reason I had talked her into trying out for basketball. She was my best friend, and I wanted her at the tryouts even if she didn't make the team.

Carla and I were different. I was good at basketball and lacrosse; she was better at field hockey and soccer. I was tall, she was short. My skin was light, hers was tan. My hair was straight, hers was curly.

I was the quick one, specializing in steals and fast breaks. But Carla was the ideal team player in every sport. She had a natural instinct for passing and she made any group run smoothly.

Our main difference, though, was our personalities. I had friends but I wasn't very outgoing. Carla knew everything about everyone in our grade and she seemed to be friends with all of them. Except...

"Lindsay Oxman will be there," Carla said. "I hope we don't get put in her group."

"Yeah. And I hope we're in the same group."

Both of us were nervous—especially me, because I was really passionate about basketball. Carla enjoyed it, but it was just something to do for fun, not a big dream of hers. She didn't shoot baskets in the cold November rain even when the ball slipped into the mud. Sometimes I envied her easygoing nature, her ability to take things so lightly.

As it turned out, Lindsay was in our group. Lindsay had hated Carla since preschool. They had been in the same class every year since they were three, and by the time Carla and I met in the first year of middle school, she and Lindsay were well-established enemies.

Lindsay seemed to have everything her way. She was pretty, athletic, and popular. Logically, she should have been best friends with Carla, who also seemed to have everything her way. But while Carla was always herself, Lindsay got her way by stepping over people, by lying, by pushing and shoving her way to the top of the social pyramid. She was the same way in basketball: a show-off and a ball hog.

First we warmed up with shooting. I enjoyed shooting—dribbling, turning, releasing, then darting to catch the ball as it fell through the net.

Next we did lay-ups. We were in two lines; one person made a lay-up and the other rebounded.

When Lindsay passed me the ball, it bounced off my foot. Maybe I was just nervous and distracted, or maybe she did it on purpose, but I could feel the heat rising to my cheeks as I chased after the ball. I couldn't even concentrate enough to make the lay-up.

After lay-ups, we did one-on-one. I was good at that—that was how I practiced in the driveway with Matt. Dribble to the right, crossover, dribble left-handed, protect the ball with your body, turn, switch hands, go in for a lay-up. On offense everything was simple. And then on defense, quick little steps, hands out, watching the stomach in case they try to fake with the head, forcing them to their weak side, waiting for them to hesitate, and then reaching out to steal the ball.

It was going fine until Lindsay was my defender. I was dribbling around her when she stuck out her foot and tripped me. My knee slammed into the floor and scraped across it. The ball bounced off the wall and rolled to a stop.

"Are you all right?" she asked sweetly, reaching to help me up. We both knew that she was putting on an act for the coaches. "Loser," she mouthed at me. At least I think that's what she was trying to say. I was too busy glaring at her and trying to pretend that I was perfectly fine to pay attention to the shape her mouth was making.

I went to the back of the line. My knee was throbbing painfully. Carla caught my eye and shrugged.

We finished this part of the tryouts, and the coaches divided us into teams. Most of the tryouts would be small games, three-on-three, so they could see how we played.

Lindsay and I were on the same team. We were playing Carla's team first. Lindsay brought the ball up, but wouldn't pass to me even though I was open. She tried to make a three-point shot but it didn't even reach the basket. I jumped, caught the ball, and passed it to the third member of our team, who made a basket.

But Lindsay just wouldn't give me the ball. I spent the whole time running to shake off my defender, yelling that I was open, but not getting the ball. The few times I did get the ball I shot. I only missed once.

"What a jerk," Carla muttered during our water break. "She could at least *pretend* to be a team player."

I gulped down water and wiped my mouth with the back of my hand. "I can't really do anything about it," I said.

"Yeah," admitted Carla, "but look on the bright side. With her attitude, Lindsay'll never make it."

I nodded. That wasn't what I was concerned about. I was worried that *I'd* never make it.

Our next game went on pretty much the same way until the last minute of it. We were losing by two points (the coaches say the scores don't matter in tryouts, but I keep score in my head, and something in me wants to win.)

I brought the ball up this time, and I dribbled right up the center, stopping right behind the three-point line. I bent my knees and sent the ball arching beautifully towards the basket.

I thought that Lindsay couldn't do anything to ruin this for me. I could tell as soon as the ball left my hands that it would be another perfect shot.

But Lindsay was a good rebounder. She could jump higher than anyone. She leapt up to catch the ball. She snatched my perfect shot from right in front of my nose. She dribbled into the basket and turned around for a reverse lay-up.

Showoff, I thought furiously.

"Nice pass," she remarked afterwards, as we were leaving. "A little high, though. I always prefer bounce passes myself."

I clenched my fist as she walked away. Carla didn't say anything. Someone else might have told me to ignore Lindsay, but

Carla understood, and she was probably as angry as I was.

THE TRYOUTS were on a Friday. The coaches would call you by the next Monday if you were on the team.

Ten long days of waiting began.

I spent the waiting time shooting hoops, three-point shots over and over, endless lay-ups, just hoping that somehow practicing now would get me on the team. Carla didn't come over; she was busy. Matt didn't offer to practice with me. He had waited before, and he understood that waiting must be done alone.

Lindsay smiled smugly at me in the hallways. She thought she would make the team and I wouldn't. But as the week wore on, the smiles grew less frequent and less smug; she was waiting, too, and she hadn't received the phone call.

I waited. The call didn't come.

"It doesn't matter," Carla said. "You're still the best player in the school. It's not your fault that Lindsay's a jerk and coaches are blind."

On Thursday they called Carla. She biked over to my house right away. She had to tell me in person.

"That's great," I said when she told me. But I felt somehow cheated, betrayed, and my voice was hollow, my smile forced.

"It isn't fair," she said. "I only went because you wanted me to. I'll talk to the coaches about Lindsay. It'll be OK."

I doubted it, but I didn't say so.

The next day in school I arrived at first period and saw someone's notebook on a desk. I recognized it immediately; it was Lindsay's. "Where's Lindsay?" I asked when the teacher came in.

"She went to get a book from the library," he told me. "We have silent reading today."

He left to stand in the hallway and yell at kids. I got out my book, but I kept looking at the notebook.

Suddenly I shut my book and reached for the notebook. Here was my chance to get even at last. My thoughts of revenge were vague, but this was a time for action and instinct, not for thought. I seized the notebook and flipped it open.

It was a spiral notebook, almost full by now, the pages filled up with orderly scribbles in blue ink, full of everything Lindsay had thought since September.

I could hear Lindsay talking to the teacher in the hallway. I scanned a page near the middle and tore it out. When Lindsay came in her notebook was sitting innocently on her desk, and I was reading almost as innocently at mine.

The folded paper sat like a lump of coal in my pocket all day. My conscience and curiosity nagged at me, causing me to be unusually quiet. Carla thought it was just because of the basketball team.

"Cheer up," she told me. "They could still call in the next three days."

I didn't answer. I didn't want her to know what I had done.

As soon as I got home I went to my room and shut the door. I tossed my backpack on the floor, sat down on my bed, and took the piece of paper out of my pocket.

It was crumpled up because I had jammed it into my pocket. I smoothed it out against my jeans, but for a moment I didn't look at it. Instead I stared at my backpack on the floor, half thinking about how its bright blue stood out against my cream-colored rug, half thinking about the note.

I wasn't sure what exactly I expected to find. I had seen Lindsay writing in her notebook many times, but I didn't know what she wrote. I smoothed out the paper again and began to read:

Everyone else has a best friend—someone they talk to, someone they do everything with. Everyone has someone they can rely on, but I don't. I hate having so many friends, because I think they all secretly hate me.

Best friends tell you what people say about you, but I can only guess about the things people whisper behind my back.

Brianna's so lucky to have a best friend. I wish I had a best friend like she does. (Is it OK to be jealous of someone and terrified of them at the same time? It's all so easy for her. I try so hard to say hello to her, to smile at her in the halls, but she just hates me so much.)

The tryouts are coming up. Brianna has a best friend to come to the tryouts with her. A lot of my friends are going, but they've already sorted themselves into their own little pairs. They're not real friends. They sit with me at lunch and discuss fashion with me, but they don't really care about me. I don't think anyone does.

I really want to make the team. Basketball's the only constant in my life. I want to shoot hoops forever. Maybe if I make enough baskets it will all go away.

I STARED at the paper. What had I done? I felt sick with myself and with the world. There was an angry lump in my throat.

It was perfect material for ridicule and for blackmail. I had control over Lindsay now, and I could get even with her. Wasn't that what I had wanted? I wasn't sure anymore.

I wanted to show the paper to Carla and laugh at it. I wanted to not take it seriously, to make fun of it the way I made fun of the announcers' voices on cheesy TV commercials.

But I couldn't, because I knew this voice, and it was so similar to my own. I wanted to undo everything. If only there were some way to put the page back into the notebook, everything would be all right.

The phone rang, but I barely noticed it. All I heard was the crinkling of the paper as I crumpled it into a ball. I stared at it.

Maybe when Lindsay smiled at me she really wasn't mocking me. Maybe she was just smiling, like everyone does. And maybe I should smile back at her.

Matt came running up the stairs and burst into my room. "It's for you," he said, holding out the phone.

I didn't understand why he was grinning so broadly, but I swallowed painfully and muttered, "OK." I sent the crumpled paper arching beautifully towards the trash can.

It was a perfect shot.

On Thin Ice

by Sean Fay, age 12

IT STARTED OUT as a clear winter's day, cold enough for a jacket and a scarf but not bitter enough for several layers of clothing. As Zach Fields walked down to the edge of the lake, he could see his breath spiraling away from him into the air. It was a quiet and peaceful afternoon.

He was just going skating, as he had done ever since he could remember. He had not bothered telling his parents, for he would only be gone for a little while. With his skates strapped over his shoulder, he approached the lake.

The lake was very large, several families besides his lived in scattered places around the water's edge. Some used it for a year-round house, but his family just visited for the holidays. He liked it better here, for the forest was all around him and he could almost feel Mother Nature close by. He knew where all the animals lived, and even named a few of them. Of course, all the forest animals were fast asleep now. Even so, he was more at home here than anywhere else in the world.

Sean was living in Camden, Maine, when his story appeared in the July/August 2006 issue of Stone Soup.

THE STONE SOUP BOOK

Cautiously, he took his first gentle step onto the ice. Testing it, he slowly shifted all of his weight onto its slippery surface. It seemed strong enough, so he quickly tied on his skates and was off.

Zach loved skating. He felt as if he was gliding across the land, without a care in the world. The gentle wind, the ease of movement, he always has and always will love that feeling. Expertly, he did a few flips and turns, stretching his muscles until they felt ready to burst. He etched a few patterns into the ice and twirled around, totally unaware that he was slowly moving away from his house. After a while, he glided to a stop. The wind had picked up, and it had started to snow. He decided to go back.

It was harder moving against the wind, so it was slow going. He had at least a mile to go until he reached his house, so he knew he had to keep going. His parents would get worried if he didn't come home soon. The sun was at its lowest point in the horizon, and the temperature had dropped. The air was sharp and brisk. Each breath sent a freezing dagger into his lungs, filling him with pain. The light snow had turned to a frenzy of sleet, pelting him in the face and making his skin raw and numb. An icy wind blew all around Zach, bringing the cold to the core of his body. He shivered. He wished he hadn't gone so far out. As he got colder, he slowed down. By about ten minutes he was barely moving. He crouched down, absorbing all of the body heat that he could.

Suddenly, he heard a creak behind him. A split second later, a groan, and then a crack appeared on the ice. It grew wider, and branched off into several smaller cracks. Then another crack appeared, and another. He sprang to his feet, and flew off. He could hear the groans of thin ice behind him, and sped up. The cracks raced behind Zach, growing and splitting and staying at his back all the while. The sleet and snow made seeing almost impossible, so he had no idea if he was even going in the right direction. Then it happened.

The cracks finally caught up to him, and in a split second had surrounded him. He was frantic. He tried to move, but every time he did the ice creaked, and another crack formed. He was trapped. Even as he stood still, the cracks came closer and closer, and in a flash he was submerged in the water.

The freezing temperature hit him like a speeding freight train. The cold penetrated his flesh and went straight to the bone. The water sucked all the strength out of him and left him weak and even colder. As he bobbed back up to the surface, his head hit the ice. Using his remaining strength he pushed with all his might, but the ice wouldn't budge. His skates dragged him down, pulling him toward the murky depths of the lake. His eyelids were stiff and frozen, and no matter what he did they wouldn't open. He screamed in fright, but only bubbles escaped his mouth. Oxygen rapidly escaped his tired body, and his lungs pounded in his chest for air. He frantically searched for an opening in the ice with his hands, but found none. A wave of pain washed over him, and his lungs throbbed faster and faster and faster. Just as he started to sink into a void of darkness, his hands hit air, and he scrambled up onto the ice.

He feebly pushed himself onto the frozen water, and collapsed on its surface. He gasped and wheezed, filling his lungs with air. Coughing, water poured out of his mouth, collecting on the ice. Shaking uncontrollably, Zach curled into a ball to find any heat possible, but found nothing. He shivered and blacked out.

When Zach woke up, he was still huddled on the ice. His clothes were sopping wet, and his ice skates were a wreck. He knew he had to move to stay alive. Hugging his dripping coat to his body, Zach made his way bit by bit back to his house. Extremely fatigued, he clomped up the steps to the back porch, and shakily removed his jacket, skates, shirt, and socks. His fingers were blue with cold, and numb. Fortunately, a fire was crackling and sizzling in the fireplace. Zach crouched and warmed himself by the fire. He made a cup of hot chocolate, and was walking back to the living room when he noticed a note on the kitchen counter. It read:

> Zach, we're out looking for you. If you find this note, please
> get warm and call us. Your father has his cell phone with him.
> We are so worried about you!
>
> Love, Mom

Zach smiled as he reached for the phone. He slowly walked
back to the couch and pulled a blanket over him. The hot chocolate was an immediate relief and filled Zach with a tingling sensation all over. As he punched in his dad's cell phone number he
thought, Sometimes, you can only rely on yourself.

Outside, the ferocious thundering of sleet had turned into a
soft, light snow, and the wind had ceased. As the sun went down,
it shed its last rays on the ice. It shimmered and gleamed in the
last fading rays of the day, and then darkness enveloped the land.
Peace and quiet reigned once more.

The Swim Test

by Samantha Cecil, age 12

"IT'S GOING TO be cold," laughed Riley. "I'm warning you, when I took the swim test, I almost froze. They had to defrost me."

"Thank you for sharing that wonderful piece of moral support with me," I snapped. Riley had been coming to Camp Walton's Grizzly Lodge for seven years now, since she was five. It was my first year. All the first-year campers had to take the swim test, to be able to swim outside the four-feet line and to go waterskiing and wakeboarding. I definitely had to take that swim test.

I had no worries about the test until I met Riley (actually, only twenty minutes ago). I was on the swim team at my school, so the four laps would be a piece of cake. (So I'm in the slowest lane; I can still swim, can't I?) And treading water for thirty seconds would be no problem, since I was a goalie for my school's water polo team. (It was my first year, making me the worst goalie, so I had to have more training, but everyone at Walton's doesn't know that, do they?)

Samantha was living in San Carlos, California, when her story appeared in the January/February 2006 issue of Stone Soup.

THE STONE SOUP BOOK

We walked down to the edge of the lake, along with Riley's little sister, Quinn. Riley was silent because she knew she'd scared me about the whole swim test thing. Pools were *heated*. Lakes *weren't*. Finally, as we neared the opening to the sandy beach near the lake's edge, I said, "Riley, it can't be that bad. I mean, they wouldn't make us swim in forty-degree water. Your memory must be malfunctioning."

"Then take it from me," said Quinn, talking for Riley. "I only took it four years ago. The lake is *cold*. You'll die as soon as..."

"Quinn, we are here for moral support," interrupted Riley, shushing her sister. "Do not frighten her to death."

"No, that's what *you're* here for," grumbled Quinn irritably, but Riley didn't answer as we entered through the small gate between the overgrown bushes. Everything *looked* normal; the sand was fine-grained, yellow, and easily got between your flip-flop and your foot. The lifeguard, Brian, and another bored-looking boy of about fifteen were manning the swim area. Brian was sitting cross-legged on the diving board. And beyond him, the water looked anything but deadly. It was deep azure and sparkling as the sun's rays danced on it. Everything looked fine to me.

Upon seeing us, Brian jumped up and exclaimed, "Finally, people are here! What are your names?"

I said, "Samantha, or Sam."

Riley answered, "We are here to hold Sam's towel and attempt to save her when she dies of hypothermia."

"Moral support?" muttered Quinn.

Brian smiled. "Don't listen to them. Just swim four laps, there, back, there, back," he indicated with his clipboard, "and then tread water for thirty seconds."

"Good luck!" said Riley. "We'll cheer you on if you start to develop swimming difficulties."

"I told you, I was on the swim team, and a water polo goalie," I said, stepping out of my shorts and T-shirt to reveal a blue bathing suit with hibiscuses all over it. "How hard can this be?"

If only I knew. My first step into the water wasn't that bad. My toes kind of curled back, like when you step into the shower and the water isn't quite warm yet. Then my next step brought me underwater to my knees. My calves tensed. That was kind of cold. A shiver ran up my spine. Then I stepped farther, up to my waist. My legs were *cold*. Oh, they were cold. The next step brought me considerable shock and pain. I was all the way up to my collar. It was as if a giant eel wrapped around me and shocked cold waves all through my body. I was frozen. My breath came out short and ragged. I could feel my blood temperature dropping rapidly.

I turned around and mouthed soundlessly to Riley and Quinn. What I meant to say is, "How did you survive this? I'm going to freeze! Pull me out now, before it's too late!" but I guess my voice box wasn't connected to my lips.

"I can't help you now," said Riley, as if she understood me perfectly. "Just get it over with is the best advice I can give you. Go on."

I nodded, turned around, kicked my feet out from the muck I was standing in, and was off.

I have swum in swim meets before. You dive off a diving board and keep your head underwater. You move your arms and legs as fast as you can to get to the other side. That was not how I swam in the lake. I kept my head above water, swinging my arms in front of me as if to grab the water and pull myself along. I tried kicking like in freestyle, but it ended up being a cross between a scissor kick and a breaststroke kick, a sort of jab at the water that I repeated again and again to get myself to the other side.

When I reached the other side, I was shivering uncontrollably. I was afraid to go back across, but it seemed I had no other alternative. Halfway across the second lap, my chest started to seize. I felt like the giant eel was back again, squeezing my ribs together and allowing no air to come out. I had to stop dead. I gasped for air. Panic was filling me, taking the place of all my energy. It weighed in my stomach like a cold lump of steel, dragging down not only my physical body but my sanity and chances to get to the other side. Fear was coming in now, filling my mind with horrible possibilities, and taking over that part of my brain that makes decisions. Fear was the blackness growing at the edges of my brain, eating me away. My body was growing numb. The world started to spin. Vaguely, I heard girls' voices shouting, but I couldn't really pay attention. My brain was having a seizure and my heart was going to explode.

It was at that point that somewhere, deep inside my body, a little passage opened. That passage held the only energy left in my body. I spurred myself on, throwing myself at the water and hurling myself forward. My brain cleared. The world stopped spinning. I gulped down air the best that I could. When I reached the other side, I quickly stood up in the muck that was the lake's bottom. The giant eel disappeared. I gasped and choked, and spit out water. Riley, Quinn, and Brian were cheering. Brian said, "You're halfway there. Good job. I bet it's cold."

"You don't even know," I murmured, and dove back in.

Gasp, choke, thrust legs, pull with arms. Gasp, choke, thrust legs, pull with arms. I moved like a frog with a broken leg. But if I kept breathing evenly, the giant eel couldn't get me. I still vaguely felt my chest being squeezed, and air was definitely harder to breathe, but I just endured. If I made it through, I never had to do this again. If I didn't—well, let's just say the giant eel would take me.

After the third lap, I think part of me knew I was on the final stretch. I looked up one time and saw about a dozen kids, along with Brian, Quinn, and Riley, cheering me on. Four other kids, wrapped in towels, watched me intently, to see whether I was dead yet. No doubt Riley gave them a great dose of her famous moral support. At this point, I didn't care. I just wanted to get out of this Arctic wasteland and erase it from my memory. I actually kicked my legs. I moved my arms more syncopated, instead of flailing them together. When I reached the diving board Brian was crouching on, he smiled at my shuddery breaths and odd swim stroke—part freestyle, part breaststroke, part doggy paddle. He said, "Good job. You're done with the laps. How're you feeling?"

It may be a standard question, but did he notice that my face was practically blue? "Cold," I squeaked.

"Well, just tread water for me and you'll be out of the cold."

I had never been so glad for the hours of grueling training I went through. Because it was my first year as goalie in water polo, I had to adjust to something called an eggbeater, a fancier way of treading water. You pretend like you're sitting in a chair and move each leg in a circle and at a different time, like an eggbeater. I spent practice after practice with Nikki, the best water polo goalie in high school water polo that year, and she had me practice and perfect my eggbeater. Now here, in the freezing lake, when Brian said the words "tread water," I began eggbeatering. Just like that. I didn't even know what I was doing at first, because it had become so natural to me during water polo season. It gave me enough time to look around at the other kids, who were eyeing the water rather apprehensively. I didn't blame them one bit.

"All right, Miss Sam, 3-2-1, done! You passed," Brian informed me. "I liked the eggbeatering. It was done well."

"After hours of it every day, it would become natural to you too," I snapped, trying to communicate to my muscles that I could get out of this melted ice trap.

When I finally managed to get out of the lake, Riley handed me my towel, grinning. The air was actually burning my skin, and I remember it being rather chilly down by that lake. "You passed that when you were five?" I asked, massaging my goose-bump-sprinkled arms. "I almost froze. I was afraid you were going to have to chip me out of a block of ice!"

"It took me about forty minutes to pass," Riley replied. She took my hand and pressed it against her cheek. "Oh my goodness that's cold!" she screamed. "I forgot exactly how cold it was!" She led me over to a reluctant-looking little girl by the water's edge. "This is how cold you'll be after you get in there," she said, pulling my hand to the girl's cheek. I yanked it away.

"Remember, Riley," I teased. "You're supposed to be here for *moral support*."

THE STONE SOUP BOOK

Basketball Season

by Rita Rozenbaoum, age 12

Week One

I ROLL DOWN the car window. It's hot. The engine murmurs
steadily. I can feel my stomach flipping as we near Fullor. The
basketball courts loom ahead, all empty but one. The two-door
Toyota stops. Amy jumps out quickly. I take my time, slowly stepping out onto the scorched cracked blacktop. I can feel the heat
through my black sandals. We wave good-bye, and I force a smile.
Inside I am whimpering.

Amy jogs over in her running shoes, short brown hair tied
back. A blue sweatshirt casually blends into relatively baggy jeans.
I wobble after her, my shoes slowing me down. I had curled
my hair the night before. It lay like a doll's. Big hoops dangle
from my ears, giving way to a silver choker necklace. It was all
planned out the night before. The clothes. I wanted to make a
good first impression. Tight jeans match with my tank. It reads
"Princess."

We stop in front of the coach. He frowns at me, observing

*Rita was living in Arcadia, California, when her story appeared in
the September/October 2002 issue of* Stone Soup.

my ensemble. I can feel my face turn red. I didn't know they would all be boys. Sixteen boys. Sixteen pairs of eyes. Sixteen smirks.

We need to run a warm-up lap around the bare field. The boys gradually pass me. Sympathetically, Amy matches my slow pace. I stare longingly in the direction of home, but am forced to turn a corner and head for the sneering crowd instead. A ball rolls out toward me, slowly. I pick it up. What am I doing here? Who am I trying to fool? Being on a team seemed like a great idea two weeks ago when I applied. But now, as I look around me... I just don't belong... I close my eyes, in hope that I can just wake up from this bad dream ... They open, looking down. I hold in my hands a basketball. I drop it, watching it roll away. Slowly, I turn to run.

We both slip on the gravel. The boys make no attempt to muffle a loud laugh. I know they're laughing at me. Amy goes to Felton Junior High. Fullor and Felton are like brothers. The two schools end in the same high school. They accept Amy as one of them. I am the outsider at Remdon Private Middle School.

I arrive last, panting loudly. Everybody stares at me, annoyed. I held back the group. Coach says something about an all-star team. "The judges will choose the two best players... It's in your hands... Only those who really want it..." I am not listening. A boy with mousy brown hair and large front teeth whispers something to his friend. Distinctly I can make out the words "pathetic" and "blondie." They snicker, causing the coach to clear his throat loudly in their direction. I stare down at my feet. The private whimpers inside of me are threatening to reveal themselves to the world. The only pathetic blond here is me.

Week Two

I FEEL MY forehead. It seems fine. I stand still and close my eyes, searching every inch of my body for any sign of pain or illness. If I concentrate really hard, I can almost feel some pressure in my head... It's useless. Unfortunately, it seems I'm in perfect health, and basketball practice starts in fifteen minutes.

Week Three

I DON'T KNOW if it is the boys' taunts or really just my lack of ability that is causing me to miss. Every shot. Insults are murmured constantly in my direction, loud enough for me to hear, yet concealed from the coach. Things like "princess" and "loser." I don't dare tell him, for fear of what the rest might do to me. It doesn't make the situation any easier to accept, that apart from Amy, I am the oldest.

No matter how much older I am than the boys, I'm still too young to have a nervous breakdown, but I fear it is edging close. Sobs echo throughout the inside of my head. My life is turning into a living nightmare. Amy gave up trying to convince me to ignore them. Ignore them? How can I just ignore them? Easy for her to say; feet don't stick out in attempts to trip her as she walks by. Every little mistake of hers is forgotten automatically. Mine are as good as posted for public viewing.

Week Four

SHOOT... MISS. Shoot... miss. Shoot... miss.

Week Five

THE BOY with the big teeth goes by: C.J. Every now and then I make a shot. Nobody notices.

Week Six

C.J. SAYS he'll give me a dollar for every shot I make. He coughs when I'm about to shoot and makes attempts to trip me when Coach isn't looking. So why don't I just leave? I thought about it. It's too late. If I go now, C.J. will think he defeated me. I feel like Hamlet. To leave or not to leave... I'm not the quiet accepting type. I'm proud. Perhaps too proud. I shout back the first insults that come into my head. C.J. and his followers can top anything I say. I don't care what the coach thinks, either. I don't think he even notices anything is wrong. He's far too ignorant and absorbed in his own little world.

C.J. says something about my school. I throw the ball so hard at him, he falls over backward. Coach sees this as an accident. With their "chief" gone for the day, the boys don't seem to find any pleasure in making my life miserable. Only a fraction continue to taunt me. Today I made my first three-pointer.

Week Seven

I AM WEARING sports pants today. My hair is tied in a ponytail and I have no jewelry. I am not the last chosen for the team today, and say nothing to C.J. He remains silent as well. I'm beginning to understand why it was so hard to move and why I wasn't fast enough...

There is tension in the air. Our game is coming up. The weather took a sharp turn from blazing sun to icy rain. We have only one real game before two all-stars are chosen. Unfortunately, CJ. doesn't cease screaming things at me. It doesn't seem to bother me as much anymore.

Coach says we can't go home until we finish ten layups. One by one my teammates leave. Ten people left... seven... five... three... and then I'm alone. Coach says I don't have to finish them. I refuse to leave. I pick up the ball and throw it continuously at the net.

That night in bed I dreamed of nothing but the twenty layups that I made.

Week Eight

THE WHISTLE BLOWS and the ball is in the air. It shoots from team to team. It looks fun from the bench. That's where I am and have been for three-quarters of the game. Coach forgot about me. He and the other judges are picking two all-stars from the teams. Fifteen minutes left in the game. Ten minutes. Five... Suddenly C.J. crashes into the wall. He is bleeding. I am the only replacement. The score is 44 to 44. Three minutes left. I'm in.

There are two seconds on the clock, and the score remains a tie. A bulky boy from the opposing team smashes into me. I am fouled.

I step to the foul line. Raindrops fall silently around me. The court blurs slightly. Everything slows down, almost as if the world were paused for that brief second of time. I hold in my hands a basketball. And then it's not the crowd of laughing boys... it's not the annoyed looks... it's not the insults, and the mockery... it's just me and the ball. Nobody else is there. There is no body in the world but me and my foul shot. The judges are watching me... somewhere... It is all so simple. Tomorrow I will be an all-star. I aim for the basket and shoot.

Flying

by Margaret Bryan, age 12

Starting Line

I ROLL MY head from side to side in an attempt to be nonchalant. My teammates look at me questioningly, and then ask, "Can we go now?" impatiently. I nod vaguely, lead them in a jog for about thirty meters, then turn around and run briskly back to the starting line. Once there I straighten my tie-dyed knee socks and perform an exaggerated walk in place. I glance at my teammates, making sure only five of our runners are in the front row and checking to see that everyone's shoelaces are tied. I focus my gaze ahead as a man walks out before the competitors and gives a brief introduction, giving the usual instructions of there being two commands, one which is vocal, and then the sound of the gun. The man disappears in the herd of runners, and another walks out.

He utters the familiar phrase of "runner's set." There is a brief pause, and then the resounding sound of a pistol pierces the air. I am off.

Margaret was living in Holden, Maine, when her story appeared in the March/April 2007 issue of Stone Soup.

Running

THE SIGHT of the other runners disappears in a flash, and the grass is rolling under my feet. My sneakers are white trimmed with red, accenting my maroon socks and uniform flawlessly. I glance back quickly as I round the bend; I am already breaking away, but not quite as rapidly as I would like. I pick up my pace, knowing that once I reach the woods I may slow down to my 3K pace and compensate for my overly swift start.

I leap over the railroad tracks and head toward the pond, only slightly aware of the crowd standing on either side of me, applauding politely. Leaping over an obstacle reminds me of a book written by one of my favorite authors, and I run through the plot briefly in my head; anything to keep my mind off the rhythm of my breathing or the length of my strides, so that I may just enjoy the run and feel the wind rushing against my face. It's a chilly day, and it will be even colder in the woods, so I pump my arms vigorously to keep the warmth flooding through my body.

The pond is calm today, the water a calico sheet of tranquility. My breathing is shallow, so I concentrate on the tune of a beloved song and transform my jagged inhalation into a placid rhythm. I swivel my head, hopefully for the last time during this run, and am relieved to note that the other competitors are hardly in sight now. I relax my muscles and move briskly toward the edge of the forest.

As I enter the kingdom of greenery and timber a slight breeze rustles ever so slightly through the trees. My energy is repeatedly replenished by this mellow gust of wind, and I continue on down the woodland path before me. There are no other sounds save the languid tones of my sneakers slapping the ground with ease, and I seem to not even be aware when the terrain ascends and I begin to run on an uphill slope.

In time I see a clearing up ahead, and feel a twinge of regret that I am leaving the peaceful solitude of the forest's haven, but it is only slight for I know that the finish line is near. As I approach the source of the sunlight and the crowd standing in the midst of it I alter my running style. I allow my breathing to become slightly more labored, and increase the length of my strides, no longer placing them in front of me in a carefree and thoughtful fashion, but in a deliberate and competitive manner, trying to look as though all I have been thinking about the entire race is a blue ribbon. For I am now exiting the woodland sanctuary in which I may camouflage with my surroundings and enjoy the scenery. Now I am a runner, and am human once more. I feel pain in my legs, and a familiar sensation of exhaustion as I round the bend, and see clearly ahead of me the true definition of a cross-country course, linear and concise in its layout.

Flying

I HEAR a roar of applause as I enter the clearing, and dimly note the crowd of spectators on either side of me, some of them wearing uniforms like myself, whereas others are garbed in merely everyday apparel. There is the part of me that notices them, that is for certain. But there is another portion of my being that is oblivious to my surroundings completely. Suddenly the coldness of the day is nothing, and I no longer have to squint to shield the sun from penetrating my lashes. I no longer feel the fatigue in my legs, and exhaustion is no longer a factor. My awareness of leaping over the railroad tracks on the way back is minor, and the sight of the finish line inconsequential. I am flying, but without the need of wings. Spreading a vast drapery of brightly colored plumage is utterly unnecessary; for I am already soaring through the air effortlessly, unconscious of my environment, hardly feeling my feet hit the soil repetitively. I am impregnable.

And then the sensation is gone, and I see the finish chute thirty yards ahead.

Finish Line

I CROSS the powdery white strip on the grass at a clocking of nine minutes and eighteen seconds. I sway to the side slightly and then regain my balance, breathing deeply as I stroll down the walkway, my hand skimming the rope fencing on either side of me for a sense of support. My mother approaches on the other side of the finish chute and I greet her, bringing a hand over my brow dramatically to give her an understanding of my fatigue. A race official hands me a Popsicle stick depicting the number one, and I accept it with a brief murmur of thanks. One of my parents hands me my water bottle, and I take a swig from it appreciatively. Immediately my strength is restored, and I jog across the field to watch my teammates finish the race. Then a sudden thought strikes me.

The memory of something that occurred only a few moments ago. I could hardly call it running—more like the vague recollection of soaring through the air, like a bird in its lazy state of being airborne.

I am curious; perhaps it will happen again? Probably not, but it's possible, isn't it? It won't hurt to try and find out.

With that, I sprint across the grassy lawn once more, pumping my arms powerfully, inhaling autumn's aroma rhythmically, concentrating on nothing in particular; just letting the wind rush against my face, making myself oblivious to sound. And running just because I want to.

And as this sentence flashes through my brain, it happens. A subtle change in the atmosphere, and the sensation of feeling light and airy, the ground so far below.

I. Am. Flying.

Diver

by Rachel Stanley, age 13

JUSTINE STARTED up the steep, blue-painted platform stairs. Her bare feet plodded through cold, chlorine-laced puddles that gathered on the narrow steps. Every time her foot landed in one of them, water rippled away from her feet, and droplets cascaded down the side of the stair, glistening as they fell to the deck below.

She clutched the metal handrail tightly and stepped onto the five-meter platform. Often she would stop here and go out to the edge, where she would perform backward and forward dives, flips, and sometimes even inward dives. But today, she kept climbing—up the next flight of stairs toward the 7.5-meter platform.

Turn around. Don't do this, her instincts told her.

But I want to! her mind shouted back. Justine kept climbing. She refused to look down, though her eyes wanted to take their focus off that intimidating goal. The ten-meter platform.

Her heart thudded in her chest. She felt lost in the roar of her

Rachel was living in Seal Beach, California, when her story appeared in the September/October 2005 issue of Stone Soup.

THE STONE SOUP BOOK

breathing. As she passed the 7.5-meter mark, she was aware of how far away the splashes of the other divers seemed, how distant the lifeguard's whistle and the swim team's hands slapping the water in the other pool were. She tried to ignore the sounds.

Justine's mind spun as she stumbled up the last flight of stairs, gripping the handrail as if her life depended on it. Her foot finally touched the top step, and she felt terribly alone on the vast platform.

Inching around the wide post at the top of the platform tower, she finally peered over the railing and looked down. Through the maze of stairs and posts and platforms, she caught glimpses of the rough, gray-brown pool deck below and dark, wet heads with bare shoulders, moving back and forth. Inhaling through her nose, she turned and walked stiffly toward the edge of the platform. She felt like a zombie.

Finally reaching the edge, she knelt and then shifted onto her stomach to look down. A large, fluffy cloud drifted across the sun. Justine shivered. She could feel the breeze much more up here. With the sun's reflection gone from the surface of the water, she could see clearly to the bottom of the pool. Her throat tightened, and butterflies suddenly filled her stomach. She stood up again and paced back and forth, stopping every now and then to peek over the railing.

She was frustrated. Her head felt as if it would explode with all her anxiety of diving off and her annoyance with the coach for making her wait so long. The more time she spent up there, the more nervous she got.

At last, after what seemed like hours, she looked down again and saw the coach yelling up at her, "It's clear, Justine. You can dive now."

OK. This is it. Justine took a deep breath to slow her heartbeat, then considered. Did she really want to dive? She'd seen the other kids do it plenty of times, but she was so high… On the other hand, diving off here would be the same as diving off the five-meter platform. The only difference was that she'd fall farther.

Almost without thinking, Justine slowly raised her arms. She paused a moment; then, bringing her arms down quickly and back up, she rose on her tiptoes and let herself fall forward.

As she dropped rapidly toward the water, she took in everything: the blue sky, the shimmering pools, the coaches, lifeguards, and swim instructors pacing the deck, the splashes of the swimmers and the other divers, the birds flying overhead, the springboards bouncing, the sun on her face, the wind in her hair... Wow! It was almost like flying.

Suddenly Justine didn't want this moment to end. She felt as if she could soar away with the birds, if only the water wasn't rushing up at her so fast...

Splash!

Justine entered the water perfectly straight and smooth, the image of an Olympic diver doing a perfect dive.

THE STONE SOUP BOOK

The Moment of Decision

by Kevin Zhou, age 13

"**S**TRIKE THREE!"

The quarterfinal game was over. Jesús Castillo had tossed his fourth perfect game in a row, earning the Little Leaguers of Miami a bid to the semifinals of the Little League World Series. His face was all over the newspapers. Headlines of Jesús becoming the next Koufax streaked across the tops of the pages. Even though it was in the Little Leagues, when was the last time any pitcher struck out every batter he faced in a game?

As Jesús was leaving the locker room, a man in a polo shirt he had seen on TV ran up to him and shook his hand.

"Congratulations, Jesús," he said. "I'm Harold Reynolds from ESPN, and I was wondering if I could do a quick interview with you."

Jesús timidly nodded his head.

"I got to ask you this, little man. What's it like being the most famous twelve-year-old kid in the country?"

Jesús felt his heart drift into his throat. Trying to find an

Kevin was living in Danville, California, when his story appeared in the September/October 2003 issue of Stone Soup.

answer, he found his mouth saying the words, "It's great."

"Tomorrow's the semifinal game. You must be nervous."

"Yes," Jesús agreed.

"Jesús, scouts from the Yankees, Mets, Athletics, and Rockies will be at tomorrow's game and the championship. Just about every scout from every team will be watching these Little League games. Do you have anything special up your sleeve?"

"No," Jesús replied. "I'm just going to pitch like I normally do."

Harold Reynolds laughed. "I know you're twelve years old, but there is talk around the league that you'll be the number one pick in the Major League Baseball draft someday. How does that make you feel?"

"Great," he answered.

"All right, Jesús, I got one last question. How did you get such an incredibly strong arm? I mean, it defies the laws of physics that a kid your age could have such a powerful arm."

Jesús could not answer that question. He simply looked into Harold Reynolds's eyes.

"It's all right," Reynolds said. "Your secret can stay a secret. Anyway, thanks a lot for giving us your time to do this interview. Good luck in tomorrow's game." With that, he left Jesús. For ten minutes, Jesús sat in his chair, looking at the ground, thinking.

"PLAY BALL!"

Team Miami was up to bat first. Jesús anxiously sat in the dugout, waiting for his opportunity to go out and pitch. Yet the look in his eyes was not that of the predator, but that of the prey He sat back and closed his eyes. As Jesús sat in the dugout with his eyes closed, he felt a tap on his shoulder. He glanced at the scoreboard and found out that Roberto had hit a home run.

Jesús was not the only superstar for team Miami. His best friend, Roberto, the catcher, basked in the glory that Jesús also shared. For a league of twelve-year-olds, Roberto displayed incredible power. In the previous three games that the Miami team had played, Roberto had hit five home runs. The team from Miami was truly blessed to have these two remarkable players on the same team.

Anyhow, it was time for Jesús to go to work. That inning was a breeze for Jesús. To the delight of the capacity crowd, he struck out all three batters he faced. Strangely, he did not feel any satisfaction with what he accomplished. After each batter that he struck out, he did not feel joy, but anger. His heart was heavy. He returned to the dugout, and sat in the same exact spot that he had left. He didn't like to be disturbed whenever he was pitching.

The next inning was essentially the same for Jesús as the first. Before he threw each pitch, the crowd would rise in eager anticipation to see what the result would be. Even though the stadium was packed with people, Jesús could not sense any of them sitting there. To him, the only people he could see were his teammates, the opposing team, and his father. After every pitch, he would take a look at the stands and see his father smiling with pride.

Five innings had passed. Jesús had been pitching like a man on fire. During those five innings, he had fifteen strikeouts. Thanks to two home runs by Jesús's friend Roberto, team Miami had a two-to-zero lead. As Jesús made the jog to the pitcher's mound, he looked into the stands and saw his father. Seeing that Jesús was staring at him, his father gave him a thumbs up.

Jesús handled the first batter of the final inning incredibly. Three pitches and he was out. The second batter was also remarkably easy and Jesús struck him out on three pitches. The third batter, however, presented more of a challenge. Refusing to go down, he constantly fought off the pitches by fouling them into the stands. Finally, Jesús threw a curve ball that seemed to fall from the heavens. The batter swung and missed.

Every player from team Miami ran toward Jesús. Roberto ran from home plate and embraced Jesús. He had pitched one of the most memorable games in Little League history.

Night had arrived, and Jesús knew that he would need his rest for tomorrow's big game. To his dismay, however, he tossed and turned in bed. He cupped his hands behind his head and lay there, thinking about times when he was little.

IT WASN'T TOO long ago. Jesús was still living in Cuba at that time. He was thirteen years old, and all day long it had been stormy. He had been inside fiddling with his glove and baseball when he heard screaming come from outside. His father quickly snatched him off the ground and left the house in a full sprint. After hours of running, Jesús and his father finally approached the Caribbean Sea. At last, Jesús understood what they had been running to. He saw a rickety boat tied with some old rope to a harbor. He came to the conclusion that he and his father were leaving Cuba.

Jesús and his father entered the lower deck of the ship. It was, by far, the most horrendous place that Jesús had ever been. Rats infested the area and flies were buzzing around meat that was still lying on the floor. There were no windows, so the room was extremely dark and possessed a pungent smell. The voyage to America had been long. After what seemed like days of traveling, Jesús's father told him that the trek was over.

Jesús's father managed to find a job washing dishes in Juan's Gourmet Mexican Food Restaurant. The job was absolutely grueling. He worked eighty-hour weeks for seven days. The pay was low, but he found a shabby apartment in a section of Miami called Little Havana. The apartment was not only small, but also dirty. Jesús befriended Roberto, a boy who lived across the street from him. They had a lot in common. They attended Diablo Vista Middle School, were born two days apart, came from Cuba, and loved to play baseball. After going to school, the two would go to the Community Park and play baseball every day.

One day, they saw a flyer mounted in a store window advertising Little League baseball. It exclaimed how tryouts for Miami's Little League team would be held that weekend. At first, Jesús and Roberto were ecstatic. After all, this could be the time where they could both showcase their exceptional talents in baseball to the world. As they continued reading, it felt as if the world had collapsed on them. On the bottom of the flyer, it said that the tryout would be held for kids age twelve and under. Jesús and Roberto's birthdays had just passed, so they both had just missed the cutoff date. Jesús snatched the flyer from the window anyway and shoved it into his pocket.

When his father got back home at night, Jesús angrily showed the flyer to him. At first, his father was also disappointed that Jesús could not participate in the Little League World Series, but then he came up with an idea.

"Jesús," he said, "perhaps you and Roberto can still play." His father left the apartment.

The next day, Jesús received a phone call from the manager of Juan's Restaurant. He angrily shouted at Jesús about how his and Roberto's fathers had not shown up to work and that they would be fired if it ever happened again. Jesús quizzically hung up the phone. Where could his father possibly be?

All day long, Jesús stayed home. He constantly looked out the window to see if his father was coming home, but he would always see nothing. It was midnight when his and Roberto's fathers walked through the door. They were both laughing happily.

"Jesús," he said, "get ready for your tryout tomorrow. Tell Roberto to do so, too."

THE NEXT DAY, Jesús and Roberto stepped onto the baseball field and saw that there were at least a hundred kids trying out. The manager of the team approached Jesús's father.

"Hello," he said. "Before I let your child and his friend try out, I'm going to have to see both of their birth certificates. Do you have them with you?"

"Sir," Jesús's father said in an ashamed tone, "I am terribly sorry, but I left those at home. It will probably take me two hours to go back and get them. I will leave immediately, but please let my son and his friend tryout."

"I'll see about that," the manager said.

The first half of the tryouts were for the pitchers.

"Number 56!" the manager shouted.

Jesús walked up to the pitcher's mound and was told by the manager to throw his best pitch, so Jesús decided to throw his fast ball. As he delivered the ball, it was thrown with such power that the cover of the baseball seemed to be torn right off. The baseball hit the catcher's mitt with a loud thud, and the manager looked at his radar gun in awe. The pitch had clocked ninety miles per hour.

Roberto's tryout was also as successful as Jesús's had been. During batting practice for all the position players, he would continually hit the balls over the fence for home runs. However, the baseballs that he hit did not merely scrape past the fence. He had even hit a few that went a monstrous 400 feet.

Just like he had said, Jesús's father came back to the baseball field two hours later.

"Sir," he said to the manager, "I am, once again, tremendously sorry. I have misplaced both Roberto's and Jesús's birth certificates and I cannot find them. What should I do about it?"

The manager held up his hand as if to signal Jesús's father to cease talking. "Jesús and Roberto are phenomenal. There's simply no other way to put it. They are the greatest baseball players I have ever had the chance to work with. I am truly thankful that I have the chance of coaching both of these wonderful kids. They can be on my team any day."

"Thank you, sir," Jesús's father said. "We are truly grateful that you are so kind."

"No," the manager exclaimed. "Thank you."

JESÚS WOKE UP early in the morning. He sensed that his heart was beating wildly. Baseball was the love of Jesús's life. Every time he played the game, he felt happy. During the course of the Little League World Series, he had not even felt one minute of satisfaction. Despite playing as well as he ever had, he felt anger building up. He knew that it was time for him to confess.

THE STONE SOUP BOOK

The first thing he did was go over to Roberto's hotel room. Roberto had given him a key to his hotel room, so Jesús entered. Roberto was still sound asleep, but Jesús gave him a nudge, signaling him to wake up. Reluctantly, Roberto opened his eyes.

"What's wrong, Jesús?" he asked. "It's still early in the morning."

"Roberto, it's time," Jesús responded.

"Time for what?"

"It's time for us to tell the truth."

Roberto sat up. "Jesús, are you out of your mind? The championship game is today. If we told everyone, all of our hard work would be wasted. We can't do that."

"Roberto, you not only have to work hard for your dreams, but you also have to work honestly. Both of our morals are too high to be doing this. There is no way that we could live our lives with this constantly lingering in our minds."

"Listen to me, Jesús," Roberto remarked, "you are my best friend, and I care about you. But you're talking crazy."

"Roberto, I know you'll do the right thing." With that, Jesús left Roberto.

THE HYPE SURROUNDING the Little League World Series championship game was overwhelming. TV stations and reporters from all over the country had come to cover the game. However, there was an unexpected change of events. The team from Miami had called for an unanticipated press conference prior to the game. The reporters flocked to the room in which the press conference was being held and saw the entire team from Miami sitting on the stage. Jesús had a microphone in his hand. The reporters settled down.

Jesús glanced at Roberto, but he turned his head away.

"I have something to say to all of you," Jesús addressed the crowd. "I have always loved the game of baseball. I remember when I was younger and played catch with my father, I felt a joy that I cannot describe. Despite the success I've been having of late, I have never felt an ounce of joy. As a matter of fact, I've felt guilt. There is something riding on my back that I must tell all of you. I am not twelve years old. I am, in fact, thirteen."

The reporters gasped. Every member of the team from Miami glanced at Jesús with shock. Every single player except for Roberto, who still was looking the other way.

"I am sorry," Jesús apologized, "for any grief I've caused to my teammates. I take full responsibility for my actions. Once again, I am deeply sorry."

The next day, Jesús woke up early in the morning after a red-eye flight back to Miami. He went outside and saw that the newspaper had been delivered already. He opened it up to the sports page and saw a huge picture of Roberto. The words "Roberto Garcia Wins the Little League World Series with a Pair of Home Runs" streaked across the top of the page. Jesús continued to read and saw that "the commissioner of Little League baseball has banned Jesús Castillo from youth baseball forever."

Jesús sighed to himself and walked back into the dilapidated apartment.

Second Try

by Adara Robbins, age 13

THE PLEASING AROMA of freshly cut grass wafts through my nostrils as I step out onto the rectangular field, surrounded by the sounds of night with only the glowing field lights to accompany me. My toe kicks forward the round orb; its black-and-white checkers become blurred as the ball rolls dizzyingly towards the goal. That white frame is like a beacon to me... a destination far away and nearly out of reach. It's been a while since I've been on a soccer field. I can still hear the sounds of fellow players running down the field, shoes kicking up mud and tufts of grass. For a moment, I see my coach standing on the sidelines, but I blink a few times and the image dissolves like a mirage in the desert. I remember the years of effort and the tryouts and the failures. I remember my last effort, my last push to success. And I remember that phone call, the coach who said I was number sixteen out of fifteen players who got accepted. After that, my memories blur—I never touched a soccer ball again, never set foot on a field again. I looked longingly for years at the players who made it and

Adara was living in Osprey, Florida, when her story appeared in the September/October 2005 issue of Stone Soup.

thought about where I could have been if... if... it was always what if...

I shake my head, clearing the painful memories away like dusting out an attic filled with spidery cobwebs. I still have not laid the soccer in me to rest and tonight, with the cool night air, feels like someone reopening a raw wound. My vow never to play again seems meaningless to me now as I stand, alone, on the gigantic expanse of green turf. I kick the ball again, picking up the pace now as I dribble a few yards more towards that beacon of white in the distance. I even try a few fancy moves, imagining an opposing player in front of me trying to steal away the precious ball. The chirps of the crickets seem to mock me as I ask myself what I'm doing here, on a night when I should be having fun with my friends. Instead, I'm practicing a sport at which I have no chance of succeeding or even making a team. In response, my feet start moving automatically—performing warm-ups that have been drilled into my mind so many years ago. I didn't even realize I had remembered them. I go faster now, my feet weaving around the ball, lightly touching its shiny surface as they perform those familiar movements. I hear the voice of the coach in my ear, telling me to bend lower and move faster. I speed up even more, any trace of self-doubt gone by now.

I soon graduate on to full-scale dribbling. I jog up the field as that checkered orb lightly dances in front of my feet. The wind rushes in my ears and I forget all about those painful memories. Right now, I'm just playing for myself and only me—not for anyone else. I finally reach the penalty box whose stark white lines stand out like a bright color among a sea of dark. Suddenly, that seemingly unreachable destination of the goal and its net doesn't seem so unreachable anymore. I push the ball out to the side, just like I've been taught, and snap my knee and foot as the ball goes slamming into the goal. I'm out of breath and sit down in front of the goal on that memorable ground, overwhelmed by the emotions that rush through me like a train speeding through the countryside. I feel tears coming and, embarrassed, I wipe them away. I didn't know I felt so strongly about soccer. When I feel ready, I get up again and perform every drill I know. I don't think about technique or speed, I just marvel at my grace and the fluidity of my motions. After what seems like a minute, I check my sports watch and realize a full hour has gone by since I decided to make this emotional journey. The crickets still chirp and the wind still blows tiny specks of grass across the lonely field as I pick up my treasured soccer ball and walk slowly off the field. I vow to return again tomorrow.

Losing Grip

by Julia Duchesne, age 13

ALEX CLENCHED his teeth as he heard his sister's taunting voice.

"Look at Alex! Look at him! He's scared to go up!"

With a swift move, Alex wiped the sweat from his forehead, pushing his auburn hair out of his eyes. He had waited all summer to come here to the outdoor rock-climbing center in Alberta, and now he was afraid to start climbing! Stalling, he adjusted the red helmet that protected his head and looked over at his sister Cory angrily. She had their mother's red hair and green eyes that were always full of reckless fun and determination. "I'm not scared, Cory," he said quietly. "I'll race you up!"

Cory looked surprised but nodded curtly and gripped the first rock. Alex copied her.

Their mum, looking doubtful, pushed back a strand of her loose hair. "Are you sure this is a good idea? Alex has never climbed before…"

"Relax, Mum," replied her daughter impatiently. "We're both

Julia was living in Toronto, Ontario, Canada, when her story appeared in the January/February 2005 issue of Stone Soup.

THE STONE SOUP BOOK

on harnesses, it's not as if we'll break our necks or anything. Could you say 'go'?"

"Oh, all right. Ready... set... go!"

Alex shot upwards. His small, lithe body twisted and turned as he reached for each new rock nailed in the artificial surface. His feet found tiny footholds to brace his body.

His belayer, holding on to the rope so that Alex would not plummet to the ground, looked at him in surprise. "The kid's good! How old is he? I've never seen someone go that fast in my life! Did you say he's never climbed before?"

Alex's parents watched their eleven-year-old son as he reached the top of the course; fifteen-year-old Cory arrived quite a few seconds after him. Alex had a small smile on his quiet face as he was let down to the ground by the amazed belayer. Cory then floated down on her harness, looking angry.

"Where did you learn to climb like that, Alex? Why didn't you *tell* me?"

"I- I didn't know I could," said Alex softly, a little scared of this unknown talent. "I didn't know."

Cory's face softened. "Well, what are you waiting for? Try a harder one!"

Cory and I are so different, reflected Alex. She's a daredevil, always pushing her luck. She doesn't care about danger, and it's got her broken bones more than a few times. I like challenges, sure, and I always push myself further, but I'd prefer to read instead. As an afterthought, he added, I wish I were more like her.

DURING THE NEXT two weeks at the Outdoor Climbing Center, Alex's talent flourished. By the last day, he was climbing the hardest courses as if they were horizontal and flat. He almost cried when his parents reminded him that they were leaving the next day. "It's not fair!" he yelled, losing his temper for one of the first times in his life. "I want to stay here forever!"

"Nevertheless, you have school in a month, and you know that we can't stay here forever, Alex," said his father.

Cory looked at her father. "Come on, Dad. Can't we stay another day?"

"No. We have to..."

Her father was cut off by his wife, who wanted her family to stop arguing. She addressed her husband sternly. "I have a compromise. Right now, as you all know, we are going to Greece because I want to see the Parthenon and the Greek islands—and the mountains. The mountains, I have been told, are wonderful, and we can let Alex do some real climbing there." She watched her son's face brighten considerably; he had almost forgotten about the trip to Greece. Alex knew every piece of information there was about the ancient Greek gods and goddesses, and he was eager to see Athens and the Parthenon ruins.

Her husband smiled and said, "I knew you would think of a solution, my dear."

"Honestly," she said to her family. "*What* would you do without me?"

Cory rolled her eyes. "Well," she said, sighing. "I suppose we *have* to see the Parthenon?" Knowing that the answer was yes, she continued. "Alex, we can climb some real mountains now!" Even though she wasn't as exceptionally good at this sport as Alex, she still excelled at it, as she did most sports. Climbing was the one in which Alex claimed victory over her.

L ATE THAT NIGHT, the sixth night that the family spent in Greece, they arrived at a small inn near the coast of Greece. They had hired a horse and cart for the trip, because Alex's mother claimed that she would not travel in cars any more than she had to. Alex grinned. His mother sometimes got carsick on ten-minute drives—a four-hour ride over the rocky roads of Greece's countryside would be torture for her. The past six days had been spent touring the sights of Greece; Alex had been in heaven, but now he was even more excited—the next day would bring mountains! The air was warm and laden with the sweet scent of flowers, and everyone, especially the children, was drowsy.

"The Hestia Inn," murmured Cory sleepily as she saw the small wooden sign hanging on a post. "And down that lane is Artemis Inlet. What is it with these people and the old Olympian gods?" The moment she said it, she regretted it; closing her eyes, she winced slightly as her brother opened his mouth indignantly.

Alex started to talk a mile a minute about Artemis and Hestia. He explained that of course an inn would be named after Hestia, the goddess of the hearth. The owners might want their fire to be always bright and warm, and as Hestia had tended the fire of Mount Olympus, it stood to reason that she would be the one the ancient Greeks called on when they named inns with fires where travellers could be warmed. Perhaps these people were just carrying on the tradition? He told Cory how Artemis had asked her father, Zeus, never to have to marry and for other things: a bow and quiver and a band of nymphs to be her maidens. He loved the myths behind the Greek goddesses—he said they were more interesting, and their beginnings stranger, than the gods. The Greek gods, goddesses, Muses, Titans and nymphs were the one thing he liked to talk about with other people; other than that he kept to himself.

Cory glared at him. "I didn't ask you, twerp," she said.

Alex grinned impishly and stuck out his tongue. "I don't *need* your *permission* to speak, Cory." He quickly ducked her swipe and whispered, "Be careful. The man driving the cart is Greek. They probably don't like to hear the old gods and goddesses made fun of."

The old man pulled the reins good-naturedly to halt his sturdy horse. "It is all right, little lady." Obviously he had sharper ears than the two siblings had guessed. "You could not know all of the old gods and goddesses, and it is true many places are named after them. Take Mount Apollo—it rises straight out of the water in the inlet named after Artemis. The moon always shines on the inlet, the sun on the highest point of Mount Apollo. They are always together or close to each other, for they are twins, and each place has the sun or moon—Artemis for the moon and her brother for the sun."

"Well," countered Cory, "that's all very well, but you can't say one of us knows nothing of the old gods. Alex is practically Canada's leading expert on Greek mythology."

The man bowed politely. "True, ma'am. He is a very clever boy." Then, turning to Alex's father, he said, "The Hestia Inn, sir. It is where you are staying. Did you pay at the airport, sir? Yes? Good." He tipped his hat to Alex's mum.

An unexpected yawn came upon Alex as the weary family climbed down from the man's cart and took their luggage from the back. Alex and Cory stopped to stroke the pony's smooth coat. Then they turned and trudged up to the door of the low white-stone building. The interior was cool, calm and welcoming—a gladly accepted change from the hot air outside the door.

THE NEXT DAY they were up early. Alex begged his mum to let him go climbing in the mountains of Greece; in the end it was decided everyone would go. Alex's dad sighed and ran a long hand through his dark hair. "My dear," he said, addressing his wife, "I think we have bred a mountain goat."

Alex knew that his dad didn't really mind, though. He was a kind man who loved his family more than anything else and would do anything for his children or his wife.

They met up with their guide at nine in the morning outside the inn. His name was Alen Vardalos and he brought his daughter Marisa with him. Marisa is a nice name, thought Alex. It definitely isn't as common as Alex—lucky Marisa!

Mr. Vardalos, who said he was to be called just Alen, was tall and thin—he was obviously a hard worker. He had a dark complexion and, though he smiled rarely, his grin was broad and his teeth were as white as all the other Greeks'. Marisa was ten, just a month younger than Alex. She was small and slim, with long dark hair tied back in a plait and wide brown eyes that flashed with mischief. Unlike her father, she often grinned—she seemed to have unquenchable cheerfulness.

"Well, you say that you like to climb. There are mountains and cliffs down by the coast—perhaps that is where you would like to go first?" Alen spoke quietly, and after some discussion the group of six walked down to the coast, a short half-hour walk.

At first, Alen and his daughter seemed unsure of whether Alex was strong enough to climb the low cliffs around the water line, but when he shot up the hardest path without relying on his harness, all traces of doubt were removed from their minds. They spent the whole day climbing, and Marisa proved almost as adept as Alex in reaching the top of the cliffs quickly. Alex noticed that Marisa was constantly singing one song, very softly, and that she had a very good voice. The song was "Losing Grip," and Marisa evidently had it stuck in her head.

"Girls! Alex! Time to come down! It's getting windy and we have to go back to the inn!" called Alex's mother. Sighing, Alex took one last look around him at the far-reaching view from the top of the cliff, revelling in the feel of the wind whipping at his cheeks, and climbed down to the solid ground.

OVER THE NEXT wonderful seven days, the trio formed of Marisa, Alex and Cory climbed every mountain within a hundred miles of the cozy Hestia Inn. Alex and Marisa formed a lasting friendship—they discovered that they shared some of the same interests, like Greek mythology. Artemis in particular fascinated Marisa—she had learned at an early age to use a bow and arrow, and so thought of Artemis as the goddess most like herself. It was not an uncommon sight to see the two walking around the inn, arguing good-naturedly about or sharing different versions of myths.

The last day came—the day before Alex and his family packed their bags and headed once more to the airport. The two families decided to climb the steep island of sheer rock that rose out of the Artemis Inlet.

When they arrived, they rowed over to the island in a small boat. The adults sat on the small beach on one side of the island

and Alex looked at the climb. It was steeper and smoother than he had thought and he considered putting on his safety harness. He decided against it and climbed up, securing a harness rope at the top for Marisa. He was about to put on one for Cory as he yelled, "Cory! Marisa! Put on your harnesses—it's really steep!"

"All right!" called Marisa, dropping down to earth from a meter above the ground and putting on the harness. "Cory! Come down!"

"Nah! I don't need a harness. I can get to the top fine, and the other side is easy enough to walk down when I'm done. So there." Cory continued climbing, regardless of the danger she faced.

Marisa shook her head and quickly climbed up. She was able to wedge her body into a small crack that Cory couldn't manage, and reached the top first. They were at least a hundred feet up, she realized. Then she thought, Cory better not fall! The thought was a joke—of course athletic, smart, indefatigable Cory wouldn't fall—but then she heard a grinding noise. The section of rock that held Cory was slipping—falling . . . "Cory! Grab hold of something!" she screamed, whipping around to look down. The picture of the rock sliding from underneath Cory's hands flashed again and again in front of her horrified eyes.

ALEX SAW CORY grab hold of a spar of rock and pull her body free of the sliding rock. The rock fall stopped as quickly as it had started and Cory struggled to regain her balance and her hold on the rock.

"My palms are sweaty!" she yelled. "I'm slipping!"

Alex's reflexes acted quickly as he lay down on the flat area at the top of the mountain and reached his hand out to her. "Grab hold of my hand! Don't fall!" He looked back at Marisa, who had climbed up faster than Cory and was taking a piece of rope from her pack. "Come on!" he shouted. "I've got to reach her or she'll fall!"

Marisa came over with the rope, winding it around a

promontory of rock and knotting it. "Give this to Cory," she said quietly.

Alex was surprised at her calmness—it seemed she had the situation under control. He guessed that she had probably done this before, but thought that she had to be close to panicking, as he was, so he took the rope from her and dangled it as close to Cory as it would come. "Get hold of the rope!" he told her, hoping she would not panic as well.

Alex saw Cory take a deep breath. Then, with one hand, she let go of the spar of rock she was holding on to and grabbed the rope. She was now in a difficult position, if possible worse than before. Her hold on the rope wasn't steady, and only one foot was touching the small ledge of rock she was on. He groaned, but watched Cory try to twist herself around. She succeeded. I should have known she'd be fine, grinned Alex. She could probably hold on all day.

His relief came too soon, however—Cory made a swift grab for the rope and suddenly her full weight was resting on the rope. In horror, Alex saw the rope slither out of the knot.

Marisa blanched and froze. Alex threw himself down and caught the rope—he just stopped Cory from falling to the sharp rocks below. Now he had her full weight resting on him. He dug his toes into the ground and held on.

For the first time, Alex heard his mother's voice.

"Alex! Alex! Marisa! Help her! Don't let her fall..." Her voice trailed away into silence, and Alex heard crying.

Marisa came to help Alex with the rope. "We've got to hold on to her and pull her up to a ledge," she explained, voice strained with tension.

Alex nodded and the two started to pull Cory up to a small ridge about ten feet above her and thirty feet below the top of the mountain. It took a long time and Marisa started singing the song again.

"I'm starting to trip, I'm losing my grip, and I'm..."

She was cut off by Alex. "Umm, Marisa, I don't think that's

the best song for this particular moment…"

Marisa grinned and ducked her head. "Oops. Sorry," she said, her dark eyes twinkling.

Cory's voice floated up from where she was hanging. "Who tied *that* knot?" she yelled.

Marisa looked at her feet. "I'm sorry. I wasn't thinking—it was the wrong type of knot," she yelled back.

"That's OK," said Alex cheerfully. "At least you *can* tie knots—I hardly even know how to. Just don't try to kill Cory," he said. A thoughtful look came into his eyes. "On second thought, we could just leave her here …"

"Definitely *not!*" Cory's voice made Marisa jump and she deftly tied a second, surer knot. Now Cory could climb up, aided with a rope that wouldn't break or slip from the knot. Alex watched his sister wrap the rope around her waist and start climbing, finding small hand- and footholds to brace herself with. When she got close to the top, he reached a hand out to her, but she shook her head, saying that she didn't want to pull *him* over as well. Alex took her point and stood back as she climbed over the edge. Finally, his sister was safe.

ALEX, CORY and their parents were leaving. Alex was loathe to leave—he had never had a better time in his life, nor had he ever had a better friend than Marisa. She stood next to her father, who had come to the airport to see them off. She hugged Cory, telling her not to fall off any more cliffs. Then she said goodbye to Alex's mum and dad. They thanked her for helping to save their daughter and she said demurely that she had hardly done anything, although they insisted that she had.

Alex turned to Marisa. He was suddenly shy—he had never been good about saying goodbye, especially to *girls*. "We're going to come back next summer," he said quietly. "Will your dad be our guide again?"

Marisa nodded, her two dark braids swinging gently. "Of course he will be. I don't think he'd let anyone else take you

THE STONE SOUP BOOK

around, now that he knows how crazy Cory is. Has she ever broken bones?"

"Are you joking? She's practically broken every one in her body already! By the time next summer comes, she'll have broken a few more."

Marisa laughed. "I'll probably see you before then—I'll be watching any rock-climbing tournaments they have on television." Then she hugged Alex tightly.

"I hope," Alex said. "Goodbye, Marisa."

"Bye," she said sadly.

Alex's mother called, "Our plane's leaving, Alex. Come on!"

Alex smiled one last smile at Marisa and turned away, running to catch up with his parents. When he boarded the plane, he turned on his headphones, blinking back tears at saying goodbye to Marisa. He looked out of the window and saw her waving wildly. He waved back, but she was lost to sight as the plane taxied away. Through his headphones he heard Avril Lavigne singing, "I'm starting to trip, I'm losing my grip, and I'm in this thing alone..."

He began to smile.

The 54th Rider

by Veronica Engler, age 13

SANDRA LOOKS OUT into the crowd. Her face is firm, her lips set in a straight line. This is it—the moment she's been waiting for for nearly ten years. She pulls her hat brim down over her eyes and pulls on her gloves, worn from the hard labor back when she helped her father on the ranch. She pats the pockets on her old jeans and straightens her favorite blue shirt. Then she turns and walks to the pen where the bulls are kept.

She climbs on the bull—with help from the rodeo clowns— and begins to tighten the rope around her hand. She looks up and as she does so, sees her brother-in-law, Roger, wave at her from the crowd. She doesn't smile, just nods, and lets her mind wander to the day this all began.

IT HAD BEEN a splendid day; the sun was up and shining down on the red dust that carpeted the ranch and everything on it. She had risen early, wanting to get her chores done so she could have some time to herself.

Veronica was living in Gilbert, Arizona, when her story appeared in the November/December 2004 issue of Stone Soup.

THE STONE SOUP BOOK

Sandra had breathed in the deep smell of desert, soaking in the lovely hues of the place everyone called wasteland. Her home had never been that to her—it wasn't the middle of nowhere at all. On the contrary, it was right smack in the middle of Mother Nature and all her other children. Sandra knew she'd never leave—Arizona was much too beautiful to ever leave behind.

Sandra talked to the horses as she shoveled out their beds of hay and stocked their trough with oats. Her favorite was an amber mare brought in from the wild a few years ago. She had taken to Sandra and Sandra had eventually given her a name—Dawn.

"An' how you doin', Ms. Dawn?" Sandra had asked, giving her a loving pet on the nose. Dawn whinnied in reply.

"Yes, I reckoned you'd say that," Sandra replied, looking out the window of the barn. "It sure is a lovely day."

Sandra had been twelve then, just barely blooming into a young lady. She loved flowers and kittens, horses and little children, too. But there was one thing in her life she lived for—bull riding.

Technically, it wasn't bull riding yet—Sandra had barely been a year at riding calves. But someday she would graduate to bulls—if her sister didn't stop her first.

Sandra had just finished her chores and was taking out her favorite calf—Little Yellow Jacket—when her father and Roger appeared at the corral. Sandra didn't mind them—they often came out to the corral to talk about something or another.

Sandra seated herself on Little Yellow Jacket and bent down to whisper to him. "Give me your worst, Little Jacket; I've ridden you every time." With that, she gave his hindquarters a jab with her spurs and they set off in a whirlwind of dust and kicks.

Sandra held her hand high, trying her best to stay on. Most calves went into a wave motion when spurred, so that all the rider had to do to stay on was to move with them. Little Yellow Jacket was different—he'd twist and jump, curving his body into impossible angles and jerking to the sides when Sandra least expected it.

Somewhere in all the melee, Sandra heard Roger say to her father, "Whoa! She's good! You teach her?"

She heard her father reply, "No, she did that all by herself. She is awfully good, isn't she?"

Sandra could hear her sister, Diane, her elder by ten years, yell from the house, "Oh, you boys! Don't encourage her!"

Diane had been the girly-girl, the one who loved cooking and wanted to stay inside all day. Sandra had never been like that—she had always loved the smell of the wind in the evening and the color of the Arizonan dust on her black boots.

After a while, Sandra was finally bucked from Little Yellow Jacket's back. She got up slowly as her dad led the calf away. She dusted the red from her pants and turned to go back to the house. On the way there, Roger stopped her.

"You're good," he said.

"So you say," she answered. She was tired and her throat was aching for a glass of water.

"Would you like to go to the Championships one day?" he asked.

"Yeah, one day." She turned to go back inside when Roger called out to her.

"You could, you know!"

She slowly pivoted on her heel. "What are you saying? That I could go to the Championships?"

He smiled, a bit gap-toothed, his face sweating beneath his rusty orange hair. "That's what I said."

"But no woman has ever made it to the Championships."

"How would you like to be the first?"

Sandra was silent for a moment. "You really think I could?"

Roger's smiled widened. "Sure do."

"How? I don't even have a trainer."

"Sure you do."

Sandra looked around, as though expecting to see a trainer magically appear from behind the crates stacked against the stables. "Where?"

THE STONE SOUP BOOK

"Well right here!"

Sandra almost giggled. "A funny-looking man like you being my trainer?"

"Yes," Roger nodded. "I don't think Diane ever told you this—I think she might be embarrassed by it, don't know why—but I used to be a bull rider."

Sandra cocked her head. "Really?"

"Yes, I almost made it to the Championships, but," he shook his head, "I got out on the qualification rides. I got paired up with a really old bull—I reckon he had been all ridden out years before."

"Ah." Sandra scuffed the dirt with the heel of her boot. She understood. Riders were not only judged on their ability to ride, but also by how healthy and hard-bucking their bull was.

"Could we start tomorrow then?"

"What?" Roger looked slightly bewildered.

"Tomorrow. Could we start training tomorrow?"

"Sure." Roger and Sandra walked into the house together, discussing her new training that would begin the next morning.

THAT WAS HOW she had gotten here today.

Sandra tightens the rope that connects her hand to the bull's back and looks up into the pink faces of the crowd. They're booing and whispering among themselves. Sandra can't blame them. After all, how did a skinny, freckle-faced, frizzy-haired woman of twenty-two ever make it past the preliminary qualifications anyway? And the bull she is riding doesn't help.

Sandra brings her free hand down to pat the snorting bull, its once-cinnamon hair now graying and coarse. This bull has not been ridden successfully for nearly seven years. Out of the fifty-three tries to ride the bull for eight seconds, not one cowboy has managed it.

Sandra tenses her body, ready for the pen to open as the announcer blares, "Now, Sandra Allison riding Widow Maker!"

The pen opens and instantly Sandra is thrown into a hurricane of jerks and twists, her body wrenching and slamming into the bull's back. She keeps one hand held high, just as Roger taught her, because if her free hand touches the bull all her training and work will go to waste as the announcers declare it a no-ride.

She tries to concentrate on keeping herself on the bull's back as it twists itself into a complete circle, and a thought vaguely flickers across her mind of the day she first came to Las Vegas. It seems kind of ironic to compare a bull to a city, but that's what Las Vegas was like. So full of colors and lights, all blaring and fighting each other for your eye's attention...

Widow Maker suddenly bucks into a wave, a classic cattle move Sandra does not expect. Her head slams into Widow Maker's shoulder blades and she begins to slide off. Her head is pounding, but she knows she must stay on. With a mighty show of strength she throws her body weight to the side, letting herself slide back into position.

Quite suddenly, the bell rings out, jogging her out of her concentration. Sandra straightens as best as she can while trying to stay on Widow Maker. Now comes the hard part. She lets go, forcing herself off to Widow Maker's right side. But something is wrong. Her hand is stuck, tied onto the bull's back with coarse rope. Sandra knows this is a common thing to happen, but all the same, that does not make it any less dangerous.

Sandra tries desperately to free her hand, twisting and pulling at it until her palm starts to bleed. She is being pulled alongside the bull now, and every so often an ill-aimed kick flogs her. She has almost gotten her hand free when Widow Maker makes a sudden turn, throwing Sandra in front of his forelegs.

Sandra's cry is lost in the gasp of the crowd as Widow Maker's left hoof strikes into Sandra's ribs. The force of its blow rolls Sandra onto her back, only to be kicked again by the bull's back legs. She doesn't cry this time, merely groans as Widow Maker's hooves plow into her and he snorts and paws the ground.

Her hand is free now and as she rolls from under Widow Maker's hooves the rodeo clowns jump in front of Widow Maker to distract him and chase him back into his pen. Sandra lies there a moment, then, thinking Widow Maker might come back for her; she crawls over to the side and slowly stands up. She leans against the wall as one of the rodeo clowns brings her hat. She nods gratefully and puts on the hat, tugging the brim of it down to hide her eyes. The rodeo clown helps her as they walk back to the gates. The crowd, which has been silent except for a few scattered gasps, suddenly erupts into cheers as Sandra looks back and smiles, winking at her brother-in-law in the third row.

Persistence

by Preston Craig, age 10

JESSICA MORGAN was ten years old and was already sure she was no good at anything. Her parents were eminent historians who studied the Civil War. They each had written numerous books and articles on the subject of Civil War history. Everyone Jessica knew seemed to admire them, including Jessica herself. To Jessica, her parents appeared to have limitless confidence and skill. She, on the other hand, had never felt successful or competent at anything she tried. Sometimes, Jessica wondered how she could be so different from her parents.

One hot summer afternoon as Jessica sat reading, the telephone on the wall beside her rang loudly. She picked it up on the second ring, placing a bookmark in her book. "Hello?"

"Jessica, it's Cassie."

"Oh, hi." Ten-year-old Cassie Parker had been Jessica's closest friend for six years. The girls chatted for a few minutes, and then Cassie said, "You know my brother's old kayak? Well, we're getting rid of it."

Preston was living in Mt. Pleasant, South Carolina, when her story appeared in the July/August 2004 issue of Stone Soup.

THE STONE SOUP BOOK

"That beat-up one with the wooden paddle? Why?" Jessica was surprised. She knew he loved that old kayak. She herself had seen him using it.

"My brother Aaron got a brand-new kayak for his eighth birthday. Now my parents are dying to get the old one out of the garage. I thought because you live right on the creek and you don't have a kayak, maybe you'd like it."

Jessica hesitated. She didn't know the first thing about kayaking. What should she do? Suddenly, she heard herself say, "Sure, I'll take it. My parents have always said I could have a kayak if I wanted one, but I've never had the chance to get one."

"Now you've got a great chance. So, you want it?"

"Yes, I do!" Jessica's heart leapt. She was really getting the kayak!

"Okay." Even if she couldn't see Cassie's face, Jessica was almost positive her best friend was smiling by her pleased tone. "I'll bring it over Saturday morning at ten. Is that okay?"

"Yeah, sure! Bye."

"Bye."

Jessica hung up the phone again and considered opening her book, but she was too excited to read. Tomorrow she would have her very own kayak. Visions filled her mind—visions of herself moving silently, gracefully through the marsh creeks behind her house, cutting the water smoothly. Visions of racing Cassie time and time again, propelling herself swiftly past Cassie's red kayak, winning dozens of races.

Then the dreams were abruptly cut short.

What if she was horrible at kayaking... just like everything else she'd ever tried?

The visions changed to pictures of herself floundering in the water, having tipped over her kayak, of herself running into the banks of the creeks and getting stuck in the mud.

Jessica knew she was rarely any good at anything, and, now that she thought about it, was positive that she would be as bad at kayaking as she was at video games and tennis and soccer and everything else she tried to do.

All her friends were good at something. Cassie was a straight-A student, Ginny was the best pitcher on the local baseball team, and Lila was always talking about her most recent experiences climbing mountains. They had never been mean to Jessica when she failed to do something as well as they had done it, but she nevertheless felt embarrassed every time they looked at her, smiling kindly, and said, "Come on, Jess, you know you can do it. Just try really hard."

Jessica's mind drifted back to last April, when she and her friend Lila had gone to their hometown's annual spring festival. There, among all the usual attractions, was something new—a climbing wall. "Hey, let's give it a try!" Lila had said enthusiastically, stepping forward. Jessica had had a sinking feeling, but she had agreed because she didn't want to appear as though she were afraid to try.

As the girls neared the wall, Lila confidently stepped up to the more challenging side, while Jessica uneasily approached the easier one. They were given harnesses to put on, and began climbing.

The movements felt unnatural to Jessica. As hard as she tried, she couldn't seem to find any handholds. It seemed that she stayed in one spot forever, awkwardly attempting to move upward. Out of the corner of her eye, she had seen Lila, scrambling steadily higher.

As Jessica tentatively pulled herself up another notch, she heard a sound that made her heart sink. It was the ring of the bell from the top of the climbing wall. That meant Lila had already reached the top and was on her way back down. Jessica, convinced she couldn't make it any farther, gave up and headed toward the ground. Even now, the memory of that day made her cringe.

She was still thinking about that day, and about how she would probably have a similar experience with kayaking, when she went downstairs for supper that night. Only Jessica's mother,

Elizabeth, was at the dinner table—presumably her father, James, was still working hard in his study. "Hello, Jessica," said her mother, putting a plate of spaghetti in front of Jessica as she sat down.

"Hi. Cassie called. They're giving away Aaron's old kayak."

"Oh? Why?"

"Aaron got a new one for his birthday. Well, anyway, Cassie called me to offer the kayak to me. If it's okay, she's bringing it over tomorrow."

Her mom smiled. "I hope you'll like it."

The rest of dinner passed in silence—they were both hungry, and felt no need to talk. After eating, Jessica read her book and watched television awhile, and then went to bed, apprehensive about the next morning.

JESSICA WOKE ABRUPTLY at the insistent ring of the alarm on the clock-radio sitting on her nightstand, which read: 8:00 A.M. She got out of bed, showered, and changed into shorts and a T-shirt, and by that time it was eight-thirty. Only an hour and a half until my kayak gets here, she thought nervously.

She waited, almost hoping that Cassie would be late—but no, she arrived ten minutes early, laboriously dragging two kayaks and two paddles. "I was only counting on getting Aaron's kayak, not yours, too," Jessica said as she opened the door and stepped outside to take her new kayak and paddle.

"No, they're not both yours," panted Cassie, passing her the blue kayak and one of the two paddles. "I brought mine so we could go together in the creek behind your house. I'll teach you how to do it."

Jessica did not think Cassie could have said anything more terrible. Now Cassie would actually see her kayaking. *This is the worst thing you have ever done to me, Cassie,* Jessica thought angrily, but she grinned with a huge effort and said in a voice of forced excitement, "Awesome!"

They went down to the Morgans' dock, and Cassie held the

kayak still while Jessica climbed in hesitantly. Cassie smiled warmly at her best friend. "Come on, Jessica," she said encouragingly, confidently sitting down in her own boat. "Don't be afraid. Have you been in a canoe before?"

Jessica nodded mutely, remembering summer camp and an unfortunate collision between her canoe and a rock.

"Hold the paddle like this—no, put your hands farther apart—yes, that's right. Now push the water back, alternating which side you do it on—left, right, left, right." Jessica obeyed nervously, and found her kayak moving forward. "Now, to turn left, you paddle on the right side two or three times, and you do the same thing to turn right, except you paddle on the left side. Oh—are you okay?"

Jessica nodded, looking defiantly over her shoulder at Cassie from where her kayak was lodged, stuck in the mud. "Back-paddle!" Cassie called.

"What's back-paddle?" Jessica's heart pounded. *Please don't let Cassie have to help me get out of this,* she thought frantically.

"Paddle the opposite of what you've been doing—push forwards!"

"Oh, okay." With every ounce of determination she had, Jessica thrust the wooden paddle forward. Her heart leapt as the kayak actually began to move. *I did it,* I back-paddled! she thought, unable to believe it.

And with a few quick movements of the paddle, she was speeding down the creek again, Cassie at her side, both of them laughing hard.

THE NEXT WEEK, Jessica couldn't stop grinning. She finally felt good at something, and she was hopeful that she might even have a talent for kayaking. She'd been setting her alarm clock early and going out alone to the creek every day since Cassie had shown her how to use a kayak. She practiced in the quiet, twisting marsh, under the pale blue morning sky, with tiny pewter fish zipping around her. The only sounds were the gentle lapping of the blue-gray water against the sides of the kayak and the sandy banks of the creeks, the shrill calls of the seagulls as they dove and swerved above Jessica, and her paddle hitting the water with a soft splash. It was still and beautiful, wild and untouched, and she always felt calm and peaceful when she kayaked among the herons and minnows and big blue crabs. With each passing day, Jessica felt more confident and skilled.

By noon on Tuesday, Jessica was itching to go kayaking with Cassie again and finally called her. Aaron, Cassie's brother, answered, and knew by the simple "Hi, Aaron," at the other end that it was Jessica. He knew her voice from the many times she'd called Cassie, and handed the phone to Cassie without Jessica even having to ask him to do so.

"Hi, Jessica." Cassie sounded puzzled. "What's up?"

"Oh, I just wanted to go kayaking again, that's all. Could you go with me if you've got time?" *Please let her say yes, I want to race her,* Jessica thought.

"Yeah, sure. I'll be over in a few minutes."

"I'll be waiting on the dock."

"See you." They both hung up their phones, and Jessica raced outside and sat down on the dock, dangling bare feet into the cloudy marsh water, her kayak tied to the sturdiest board.

It took a little over five minutes for Cassie to arrive, and even less for Jessica to untie her boat, hop in, and start sculling around.

"Race you to that dock with the crab trap on it," said Cassie suddenly.

"Okay." Jessica felt confident. She was not just certain that she was capable of winning, she was certain that she would win, by a long shot.

"On your mark... get set," Cassie said loudly. Jessica tensed up, ready, arms set to move. "GO!"

And they were off, at first side by side, but then Cassie began pulling ahead.

Jessica's self-assurance that she would win lessened slightly, but she worked herself yet harder, and with a massive effort, she began gaining on Cassie.

This made her grin, but the real moment of happiness came when she sped past Cassie and, with one quick back-paddle to slow herself down, stopped.

Jessica had won.

Cassie cheered as she halted beside Jessica. "Nice one!"

Jessica blushed embarrassedly. "Thanks." She might have looked shy, but underneath that, she was bursting with pride at her skill.

JESSICA'S FATHER, James, met her in her bedroom that night. "Jessica, I saw you this afternoon, kayaking with Cassie."

She turned off the radio that was blasting rock and roll. "You did? Do you think I'm good?"

"I think you're very talented." At this, Jessica had to smile, slightly embarrassed but altogether pleased. "In fact, what I came up to talk to you about is kayaking."

"What is it?" Jessica was very curious.

"There's a kayak race for ages nine through twelve in two weeks; I read about it in the newspaper. The prize if you win first place is a brand-new kayak and paddle. It starts at two in the afternoon and it's down at the park. You might want to think about entering."

"Maybe I will," Jessica replied. Competitions weren't usually her thing, but this sounded like fun. "Thanks for telling me."

Her father started toward the door, but then turned. "You are very good at kayaking, Jessica. I think you could win that race."

"Thanks."

When her dad left, Jessica stretched out on her bed, resting her chin in her hand. She was seriously considering entering this kayak race. She was hopeful she could win, or at least come in at second or third place.

Jessica suddenly leapt to her feet. She had made up her mind.

THE STONE SOUP BOOK

She was going to enter.

THE NEXT FEW mornings, Jessica woke up at seven because she wanted to practice for the race with no one else around. Every morning she followed the same routine, laboriously dragging the kayak from the garage to the dock and speeding down the creeks.

But on the fourth morning, something happened.

Jessica was going along confidently, fast and smooth. She was full of energy and excitement—in fact, a little too full.

She was so excited, staring up at the blue sky, that she didn't notice the rock. She hit it, and her kayak flipped violently over.

In a split second, Jessica was in the cloudy marsh, stunned from the sudden impact. She was trapped underneath her upside-down kayak. She couldn't see, hear, or breathe underwater. She writhed frantically in the pitch darkness, desperately trying to get to the air that was only a little way above her. Her heart pounded in terror as she kicked and flailed her arms. She slammed sideways into the kayak, banging her arm and head against it.

Miraculously, one of Jessica's wild thrashes brought her clear of the kayak and upward. Her head broke the surface of the water, and she gratefully inhaled clean, cold air that smelled of the marsh, her clothes and hair clinging to her skin.

Gasping, Jessica shakily flipped her kayak the right way up and found the paddle. She climbed weakly in and for a moment sat there motionless, unable to believe what had happened. Suddenly, she wanted nothing more than to be away from the kayak and the marsh, as far away as possible. She began to paddle back home.

When she got home, she threw the kayak and paddle in the garage and stormed upstairs to her room. "Jessica?" called her mother, but Jessica ignored her and slammed and locked the bedroom door behind her.

Why did I decide to kayak? she thought as water dripped down her back. The memory of the darkness of the water, the inability to breathe, the utter terror, was still fresh in her mind. I won't do it anymore, I won't. I'm never kayaking again.

She was sure of that.

FOR THE NEXT two days, Jessica didn't kayak at all. In fact, she rarely came out of her room and didn't call Cassie, Ginny, or Lila once.

On the third day, Jessica's mom came into her bedroom and sat down on the bed beside Jessica. "Jessica, what's wrong? What happened?"

"My kayak tipped over when I was practicing the other day," she replied shortly.

"Oh. Well, why haven't you gone back to the creek?"

"What if I tip over again?"

"Jessica, you can't let one setback get in your way. You've got to keep going. You can't give up now. You're good at kayaking. You just made a mistake. Everybody makes mistakes, Jessica."

"You and Dad never seem to," Jessica replied, almost under her breath.

"It may seem that way to you, but it's not true. Your dad and I have both had disappointments and made mistakes. Do you know how many times I've had to revise the books I've written, or how many rejection letters your father and I have gotten from publishers over the years? It's hard not to give up, but if you really want something, you've got to keep trying. You should get out there and try again, Jessica." Her mother tried to sound cheerful and upbeat.

"I don't want to!"

"The only way you can overcome a fear is to face it. Face your fear of kayaking, Jessica. Remember, even if you lose the race, you still entered and tried."

Jessica crossed her arms over her chest decisively. No one could make her enter that race, not even her mother. "I don't want to enter," she repeated stubbornly.

"All right, Jessica, I won't force you to enter, but just remember this. Failing when you've given your best effort is much more honorable than failing without trying." Jessica's mother stood and left the room.

Jessica sat there on the bed, staring at the white door, cracked a little ajar. I still won't enter, she thought defiantly, but deep down she wasn't so sure anymore. Her mother's words kept echoing in her head.

That night, it was hard for Jessica to sleep. She tossed and turned, thinking about what her mother had said to her. There was a gnawing feeling inside her, a nagging feeling that kept telling her that her mother was right.

The next morning, Jessica decided to call Cassie. Jessica waited a moment, and then heard, "Hello?" from the other end of the line. It was Cassie's voice.

"Hi, it's Jessica."

"Oh, hi, Jessica. What's up?"

And Jessica spilled out everything, about the race and her fall from the kayak, about her talk with her mother and her feelings for the past three days. "And I'm still scared about falling out of the kayak, Cassie, and I don't know what to do," she finished.

There was silence from Cassie for a moment, as though she were trying to find the right words. And then she spoke. "You're good at kayaking, Jessica. I think you should enter."

"But I—have you ever tipped over?" Jessica sputtered.

"Yes, I have, and it scared me, too. But you've got to keep trying."

"Cassie, don't you understand?" Jessica's voice was pleading. "Don't you understand how I feel?"

"I understand, but I still think you should enter. I saw how much you like being in a kayak. You've finally found something you like. Why don't you stick with it and get really good at it? Who knows how good you could get?"

Jessica was silent.

"Jessica? Are you still there?"

"Yeah," Jessica said in a very quiet voice. "I'm thinking about what you said."

"Did I sound like I was lecturing you? If I did—"

"No, Cassie. No, it's not that."

"Then what? I'm not telling you to enter, I just think it would be right."

"I guess it would be."

"Yeah, and you're talented."

Jessica smiled, flattered. "Really? You think so?"

"Yeah, I do, honest. Go ahead, Jessica, go ahead and enter. It doesn't matter if you lose—not that I think you will, but—"

Jessica laughed. "Okay. I think I'll enter."

"Good for you. Well... bye."

"Bye."

Jessica hung up and told her parents that she'd changed her mind, she was going to enter.

As the day of the race drew closer, Jessica's nervousness mounted. She practiced for hours every day because using up all her energy in kayaking helped her forget—briefly, anyway—about the race.

The evening before the race took place, Jessica was out in the marsh at about seven o'clock, kayaking, when Cassie's red kayak rounded a bend.

"Hi, Jessica!" she called, coming closer. "I thought you might be out here. I thought you'd maybe want some company."

"Hi, Cassie! Thanks for coming! Do you want to race?"

They raced each other a few times, and then the girls began to go more slowly down the creek. The dim light of dusk shimmered on Cassie and Jessica's hair, making Cassie's sun-streaked blond hair shine and the red highlights in Jessica's brown hair stand out.

"Oh, Jessica—look!" Surprised, Jessica looked up from her lap, and gasped at what she saw.

The sun had begun to set, smearing streaks of bright, beautiful shades of pink, blue, purple, orange, and scarlet all over the sky, like a masterpiece painted by a giant hand with the prettiest colors there were. The heavens had been spread with a thousand magnificent hues, some dark, some pastel, some in between, and the sight took Jessica's breath away.

As the sunset faded to a dark blue night sky, Cassie said, "Well, I suppose we should go home. Hey, I was thinking that maybe tomorrow I could go to the race with you. Can I?"

"Sure, of course you can!"

"Thanks. See you, Jessica."

"See you, Cassie." And Cassie was paddling to her house. Jessica watched her go until she was only a rapidly moving red speck in the distance. Reluctant to leave the marsh, Jessica finally turned her own kayak around and headed for home.

AS SHE CLIMBED into bed that night, Jessica's thoughts turned toward the race. She couldn't believe she was actually entering. Jessica had never done anything like this before. Anticipation and nervousness filled her—but there was another feeling, underneath the two emotions she had experienced before. This was something Jessica had never felt. It made her want to grin confidently and boast that she was entering the kayak race. She barely recognized it for what it was.

Pride.

JESSICA WOKE the next morning with a mixture of excitement and apprehension in the pit of her stomach. She was absentminded and quiet all day; the race left no room for any other thoughts in her mind.

At one-forty-five, Jessica, Cassie, and Jessica's parents got in the car with Jessica's kayak and paddle tied precariously atop and went down to the park. When they arrived, there were quite a few children lined up along the bank of a wide, straight creek that looked to be about five feet deep. A long scarlet ribbon with red and yellow flags attached to it that was obviously the finish line had been stretched across the width of the creek about thirty meters ahead. Jessica joined the line of children, all with their kayaks in front of them, and saw that every face was taut and anxious. She stood between an extremely short nine-year-old girl who was shifting her weight from foot to foot, and a twelve-year-old boy who was trying to cover up his nervousness by acting relaxed and slightly bored. She smiled nervously at the girl beside her, and she smiled back, now hopping on her left foot.

The cry of, "Get in your kayaks, everyone!" startled Jessica. She looked around sharply and saw a man with a bright red megaphone standing close by. Jessica slid into her kayak and picked up her paddle with shaking hands, forgetting her dreams of winning the race. Cassie and Jessica's family stood nearby with the other spectators, beaming and waving at her. *Please just let me finish,* she thought, smiling feebly back at them.

"Get ready."

She eased her kayak a couple inches ahead so that she could push off easily out of the sand.

"Get set."

She tightened her grip on the paddle.

"Go!"

And they were off. Suddenly there was no time to be afraid. Adrenaline rushed through Jessica's body as she worked up speed and leaned forward, working her arms harder, the rush of air whipping her hair against her cheeks. A tangle of happiness, excitement, confidence, and hope filled her as water dripped from her paddle onto her lap, going as fast as she could go. She could hear Cassie and her parents cheering her on. Other kayakers disappeared from her mind and vision. She no longer knew or cared whether she was in the lead or not. The finish line was near. The flashy red and yellow flags were whipping in the breeze, so close, so very, very close—

And then she passed beneath them.

Jessica stopped her kayak on the bank, panting and smiling. She had done it. She had finished the race. Her parents were there to meet her, smiling, clasping her hands as she climbed

THE STONE SOUP BOOK

out of the kayak. "Jessica," said her father excitedly, "you came in second!"

"I *what?*"

"You got second!" said her mother, hugging her.

Cassie came running up, grinning broadly. "Jessica, you did it!" she cried. "I knew you could!"

"Thanks, Cassie, but you're the one who convinced me to enter and everything." Jessica was very happy. In her beat-up, secondhand kayak, only recently having gained confidence in herself, Jessica Morgan, the pessimist, the girl who had thought she couldn't do anything, had not only finished a race, but had come in second.

The man with the megaphone walked up to her. "Good job," he said. "What's your name? How old are you?"

"Jessica Morgan. I'm ten."

"Well, Jessica, that was a great race. We've got a ribbon for you."

"You do? Where?" Her heart pounded excitedly.

"Right this way." As if in a dream, Jessica followed him to the starting line.

They started out with fifth place. A tall eleven-year-old boy got that. The fourth place winner was a black-haired boy of about ten. Jessica saw that the nine-year-old girl she had stood by was awarded third place. And then came second place. Jessica could hardly believe it when her name was announced. She didn't even hear who the first place winner was.

The red ribbon was placed in the hand Cassie wasn't holding tightly. Looking down, Jessica read the gold letters. Second Place.

She had never dreamed that eleven letters could make her so happy.

CPSIA information can be obtained
at www.ICGtesting.com
Printed in the USA
FSOW02n0042051216
27938FS